Joan Marysmith lives in Leicester with her husband; her three children are grown up and live in or around London. A growing number of grandchildren are a source of pleasure and time consumption. When she's not with them or writing, her favourite occupation is travelling. Her previous novels, *Holy Aspic* and *Waterwings*, are also published by Black Swan.

Also by Joan Marysmith

HOLY ASPIC
WATERWINGS

and published by Black Swan

The Philosopher's House

Joan Marysmith

BLACK SWAN

THE PHILOSOPHER'S HOUSE
A BLACK SWAN BOOK : 0 552 99812 5

First publication in Great Britain

PRINTING HISTORY
Black Swan edition published 1999

Set in 11/13pt Melior by
County Typesetters, Margate, Kent

Black Swan Books are published by Transworld Publishers Ltd,
61–63 Uxbridge Road, London W5 5SA,
in Australia by Transworld Publishers (Australia) Pty Ltd,
15–25 Helles Avenue, Moorebank, NSW 2170,
and in New Zealand by Transworld Publishers (NZ) Ltd,
3 William Pickering Drive, Albany, Auckland.

Reproduced, printed and bound in Great Britain by
Cox & Wyman Ltd, Reading, Berks.

For my son Matt, whose philosophy is all his own.

Acknowledgements

The following books have been used in research:

Investigating the 18th century. By Alison Honey.
   Pub. The National Trust. 1995
William Morris. By Stephen Coote. Pub. Past
   Times. 1995
A Book of Historical Recipes. By Sara Paston-
   Williams. Pub. The National Trust. 1995
Victorian Tiles. By Hans Van Lennon. Pub. Shire
   Publications. 1995
The Country House. By John Vince. Pub. Sorbus.
   1994
The Enlightenment. By Norman Hampson. Pub.
   Penguin. 1968
Dialogues concerning natural religion. By David
   Hume. Originally published 1779. This edition
   edited by Martin Bell. Pub. Penguin. 1985
Essays Moral, political and literary. By David
   Hume. Originally pub 1777. This edition edited
   by Eugene Miller. Pub. Liberty Fund 1985
The Life of David Hume. By E. G. Braham. Pub.
   Vauxhall Press 1931
Hume. By A. J. Ayer. Pub. OUP. 1980
Life in the English Country House. By Mark
   Girouard. Pub. Yale University 1978

The Philosopher's House

PART ONE

Chapter One

I badly need to locate Amy, my aunt. It's all too easy to mislay relatives.

The cab from the station grumbles up the long driveway, trees swaying on either side of me, like bent pensioners battling against the squall. At last, through the rain against the window, I make out the Philosopher's House.

I hadn't expected anything so grand. Never seen anything like it in my seventeen years, except on the telly. In my world, houses come joined together, or at very least, in pairs. This house stands alone with nothing else in sight, substantially square, yet elegant. Ionic columns flank the huge black front door, rows of flat windows stare out at me like superior eyes hiding secrets of children who own ponies, and women who have control of their lives. The perfect symmetry suggests order and power, a lost world of Jane Austen. Its life inside will be a different life from mine. It will be warm with log fires, especially as it's only two days to Christmas.

Paying the driver I rush out with my small suitcase to the shelter of the portico. The rain drives in at me, stabbing and icy. Soaked already.

Somewhere inside this building is my aunt. I ring

the bell, which is large and recessed into a niche, but there's no responding jangle from within. It feels loose, as if it's unconnected. No sign of life anywhere. The wind changes, the rain attacks me from the side. I turn my cheek against the sharp discomfort. Moving from below the portico I squint through the window on the left into a hallway, but it's too dark to see anything. Then, like a missile from an invisible god, a black object whizzes past me and crashes into the ground. Back in the relative shelter of the porch I see it's a giant roofing tile with chiselled edges. It missed me by six inches. Goose-pimples rise on my arms. Try the bell again. Useless. A second tile hurtles down. It's like a bloody war.

I strike the high black front door, angry now. Where the hell is Amy? Why isn't she looking out for me? I thrust my fist against the wood and the door meanders open, croaking like a frog. It was never closed in the first place.

Inside, safe from Lear-on-the-heath conditions, and murderous roof tiles, I look round for the comfort and grandeur promised by the outside. I expect gleaming black and white tiles, plenty of mahogany, some marble. Got it wrong. Per usual. The eighteenth century lingers only in the dimensions of the hall, and the stately curve of the unpolished, damp-stained staircase with grey-bloomed mahogany rail. Tatty, scarred, greasy paintwork dominates, and the musty smell, like a deserted church. The stained hall carpet is frosted with dust. There's no furniture beyond a side-table with four plastic letter trays on top. Unsolicited catalogues litter them. From a huge plaster rose in the ceiling, large enough to once have supported a chandelier, dangles a flex with a single light bulb. The past hangs on as a frail ghost. A sad presence lingers, like the promise of a flower

12

withered in the bud. This is an unhappy house.

When Amy moved here a year ago, she told us she was living in a commune. It came out later that the arrangement is more mundane. The Philosopher's House is divided into flats, and she has one of them. That's Amy for you. Being Mother's sister and of artistic bent, a painter, she's prone to exaggeration. Amy also said we must be certain to use the postal code, because the house has two names. Its proper name is Loughnian House. That's on Ordnance Survey maps. Milo Loughnian, a philosopher, lived here in the eighteenth century, though the house was built earlier. No-one was certain then how to pronounce the name, whether it rhymed with rough (which apparently it does) or with plough or though or cough. So it become known with time, as The Philosopher's House. All AA maps give this name.

There are several doors: two are individual *front* doors with modern bells and names alongside, one of which is Amy's. Beyond it, 'The Ride of the Walküre' is triumphantly belting out. Wagner is her favourite composer. Wild and romantic. Messy in his private life. Like Amy. This time the bell does buzz. However, nothing happens. Scrolls of fluff, like phantom mice, waft lazily in the draughts that play across the space. They dance on the currents as if to lost music. Something whimsical and light, with strings, not the crashing chords of Wagner penetrating the wall.

Following my third blast on the bell, there's a surprised squeak, a clatter as Amy drops something made of china. Footsteps scurry back and forth within, as if indecisive about clearing up the shards of coffee mug, or answering the door. Eventually she appears.

From the dawning intelligence on her face I know she's forgotten I'm due today. This doesn't disturb her in the least. My aunt's the opposite of a swan. All of a

13

flurry on the surface, but calm and unruffled underneath.

'Bloody hell,' she says, 'it's Charis.' She makes up for her carelessness with an enveloping hug, squashing me against her chest like a Brazil in a nutcracker. She can be as theatrical as my mother, but usually more sincere. She stands back and considers me.

'Almost a child no longer,' she says with her usual offset vision. This is a compliment, because we all know I'm retarded by my plainness from becoming a woman as quickly as the family expects. Perhaps it's the disastrous record of my female relatives' relationships that's made me reluctant to step into the blessed state of womanly knowledge. 'You look extraordinarily damp.'

She's thrown into dark relief by the lamplight from the room beyond. Amy has dry black bushy hair, each filament independent. They seem to come from one starting-point and hang down to all points of the compass. She doesn't so much have a hairstyle as a window cut out of a curtain, for her face to peer through. Her complexion is a grey cream, not a face to tan, and her strong mouth is coarse-skinned. It's not a mobile mouth, and it only reads as a smile in conjunction with her elephant-coloured eyes. These don't change shape much either, they just fill with warmth and benevolence that floods out over you. You'd never call Amy *fat*, but she's generously built, especially round the hips.

I never understood why her husband Henry went off with Fiona, so crisp, efficient, and exquisitely groomed. Amy could never be any of these; she's gentle, incompetent, and her clothes shift around her as she moves, never getting to hang quite straight. She has more mystery than an organized woman. Perhaps the split all came down to meals not appearing on the table, and finding dissimilar socks knotted together.

'Your *mother* quite buoyant?'

'Fine.' Mother's in pantomime this Christmas, which is why I'm here. She's not quite the back legs of a cow, but only marginally superior. Says she's on stage at the De Montfort Theatre in Leicester. Like Amy, *she* mislaid her husband early on. I can't ever remember my father living with us. He's still alive, though I see him only occasionally. His main function is to pay my boarding-school fees, which Mother considers necessary for her career. I've had some very useful uncles over the years, though they're getting thinner on the ground now, as Mother lands less glamorous parts. If she gets into character parts I predict a sharp decline. Panto is the beginning of the slide. The De Montfort is *not* a theatre, it's a concert hall run by the council. They put on Christmas shows with minor stars from soaps. She claims the part's been created specially for her. An assistant cleaner to Cinderella. Leicester's nothing if not politically correct. They like to help minority groups exempt from obligations, rather than mainstream council-tax payers. In this version, Cinderella may be pregnant before the final curtain, and the prince will offer her a council house. I doubt marriage is on the cards.

I explain to Amy. 'She's got a dispensing contraption round her waist like bus conductors used to wear before the driver got to take the money. It shells out condoms.'

'Such a practical woman.'

'She's not persuaded the director yet about the condoms, but the council's ecstatic. It's rehearsals until Christmas. Then two performances a day.'

'Crikey,' says Amy. The semblance of discipline throws her.

Amy's living-room is large and must be the original drawing-room of the house. This is more like it. There's a huge window at one end, and a conservatory built on beyond. In the large fireplace, where, in the absence of a fire, some might have put a flower arrangement, Amy has her wine rack. The orderliness of the room's proportions is somewhat impaired by Amy's preference for her possessions to be on hand rather than stowed in cupboards. Books stand in precarious towers, pictures lean against furniture rather than hanging tidily on the walls, and there's an ironing-board set up in the corner. But lamps shaded with swathes of jewel-rich silk scarves cast a glow, suggest live fires and solace. Suggest happiness.

Centre stage is her sofa, draped in olive- and oyster-striped damask, nailed with showy brass studs onto a functional shape. Circular garnet squabs and gold bolsters huddle in its depths like puppies in a basket. The sofa is a focus of serenity and warmth, a sacred domain amid the chaos of Amy's everyday life. This is the way of an artist, the shafted insight, clear and pure, illuminating the grey world, informing us of what might be, but never of a formal order.

As if suddenly remembering my mother is at least tidy, for she keeps all her greasepaint in a display drawer once used to segregate print blocks, Amy optimistically shoves some unopened post under the sofa. It gets jammed. She must have filed something else there previously. She pushes me into her bedroom, which is off the sitting-room, and hands me a towel. 'Get dry while I discover something to eat.'

With closed eyes I rub my face, trying to anticipate happiness, trying to feel goodness in my world. I always imagined the first followed from the second, but experience is showing this to be an unsafe premise. Such joys are so elusive.

Amy used to have a fine palate for some of life's great gastronomic accomplishments. Chip butties. Dripping toast. Sadly, since Henry's left she seems to have cut down on fat, possibly hoping that if there were less of her, he'd love her more.

We have a meatless quiche, though she's forgotten the salad and we make do with chopped tinned carrots tossed in salad cream. 'Á la Russe,' she says triumphantly. Her wide lips quiver, give a slight upward tilt. She considers the meal a culinary success.

There's no evidence of Christmas preparations, even with only two days to go. I may not believe in God, but I do give credence to *Christmas.*

'Will you be having a tree?' This seems the kindest way of pointing out the deficiency. Not critical in any way.

'Christmas trees go with men who wear waistcoats.'

Henry often wore a waistcoat, I recall. He was tall, slim and fastidious to the point of being obsessive. Swallowed his vitamin supplements in alphabetical order, laid out his letters according to envelope size before opening them.

'We'll have plenty of significant yew and ivy. *Living* decoration. Symbolic of the earth not being dead. Plenty of greenery to hand around here. Absolutely no baubles. We'll have,' adds Amy, pausing breathlessly, 'we'll have a banquet. Plenty of time to fix it.'

'With a turkey?'

'Whatever you like, dear.' Which makes it clear there's no turkey in the pipeline yet, either.

'It will be cosy, just the two of us,' she muses, 'but so much more satisfactory if we could mingle.'

'All? You mean Henry, and my mother and current uncle?'

'No. All those who live in this house, Charis. Together, in spiritual union. Not set apart by dividing

17

walls and petty egos. We're living in a burrow which never joins up.'

With her elbow, Amy indicates the wall on the right. 'We are four households. Through there is Guy Loughnian. Poor Guy is supposed to own the house, but I think most of it's gone to the bank by now. Once a peach in its prime, he was, I understand. Desiccated now. Age and stress. It's always money with these big places. So much upkeep. Sold off the estate years ago. He's forced to let three apartments now to keep the place going. You will find all the inmates here say apartment instead of flat. It adds dignity to the air of shabbiness.'

I nod encouragingly. I'm a liver of other people's lives. They create me. Because I'm so *extraordinarily* ordinary I have no self, no image. A shadow without a casting form. It's because I'm not an actress like my mother. It's a paradox that acting makes her who she is. Amy's art creates Amy. Not the other way round. I'm nothing, so I have to absorb from everyone else. I creep under the eyelids of people. Hear their thoughts.

I remember the tiles bombing down. 'Guy has a roof problem now. He's lost some tiles. Two nearly hit me.'

'Storm damage. Do you think Guy has *storm damage*?' Her grey eyes take on a gleam, and she grabs me by the hand. 'Let's see.'

We go out to the hall, and Amy presses her face sideways against the window, swivelling her eyes in all directions to estimate how much of the roof is lying on the drive. Out of the glow of Amy's apartment, the gloom of the hall hits me again.

'Could be five or more gone. He *must* have water coming in. If Guy has a hole in his roof, we'll all get wet eventually. We could do with a communal *need*. It pulls people together.' Amy still has collective yearnings.

'Of course,' she adds, guessing what I'm thinking, 'I don't want to live in a commune, or anything like that. If you share the washing you're bound to end up with the wrong knickers. There are limits. We should see if Guy needs help.'

As we speak yet another tile crashes down and shatters on the gravel. This is how great buildings become ruins.

Chapter Two

We cross the depressing hall as two elderly women totter down the stairs. They both clutch, white-knuckled, at the banister rail.

Amy waves briefly in their direction by way of intro-duction. 'Grace, followed by Adelaide. Sisters. From the upstairs apartment.' She doesn't introduce *me* to them. This happens to me all the time, I get ignored.

'Not got loosened up yet,' calls Grace, cautiously feeling for each tread with pointed toe. 'We're in search of Cob. We've made our Christmas provision list.' She infuses her words with a biblical reverence.

'Cob?' I ask.

'Cob lives in the yard,' says Amy vaguely, making him sound like a dog.

'Poor Cob,' says Grace. 'You can't help feeling sorry for him. A kind boy, I'm sure.' There's an element of doubt in her voice.

Grace is a wispy-haired waif, if you can call some-one old a waif. Her face rumples into soft folds, like silk too heavy to crease. She wears a long Monsoon shift of aubergine wool, in which she should look ridiculous at her age, but doesn't. There's something medieval about Grace. Gothic and tears and unicorns. Yes. Unicorns. A suppressed sexuality and fountain of life. Rechannelled into sorrowing, born with fortitude. These things I know instinctively as I watch her gradually find confidence in her feet, until she all but skips down the last tread.

Where Grace is birdlike, and reminds me of Mrs Dalloway, Adelaide is portly and out of a different book. Adelaide is rigid in an emerald gabardine coat-dress, with a large white collar. Her thick legs bulge over tight matching emerald court shoes. Hair that must once have been a rich auburn is now that particular shade you can only get out of a bottle. An Alice band superfluously restrains it. Unlike Grace, she wears a wedding ring.

Amy waits until they land safely in the hall. 'Guy has problems.'

'Well, he's a man,' says Adelaide. Her voice is artificially low, silted up with what she's put down her throat over the years.

Grace puts weightless hands together, as if cradling a rescued bird. 'What's happened to dear Guy?'

'Don't ask,' says Adelaide.

'It's his upper storey.' Amy rings Guy's bell. 'Losing his slates.'

His double door is not utilitarian like Amy's, but original to the house, with ornate moulded panelling. The brassware is solid, but the paint is yellowing and chipped.

Guy eventually appears, and I feel the worse for seeing him. His lofty face could only be English, from the long, disdainful nose to the full, confident chin. Aristocratic. Élite. But marred by petulant lines, like cords trying to drag downwards his nose and mouth.

'Yes?' He stands menacingly, with jacket buttoned over what looks like a pyjama top. A smear of tomato ketchup enlivens one lapel. His trouser legs, good quality twill worn to a shine, hang in coils round the

21

shin. Difficult to imagine why he bought them so long in the first place.

'Are you all right, Guy?' Grace is full of concern, caring, gentle. She stares at the furrowed features that must once have been handsome. His eyes now are as receptive as plastic plates, yellow round the edge, and within, opaque as putty. A man lacking an inner light.

'Dear Guy,' says Adelaide, reaching up to stroke his shoulder, 'we're worried about your roof.'

'At least I give you pleasure.' Guy steps back from Adelaide's wanton grasp. 'You all hope the whole bloody ceiling's come down, don't you? Think the library might be awash. All gathering like vultures.' His voice, with those contortions of vowels where money has predetermined many generations of family, set them apart from the masses, fixes him above the rest of us. A gentleman is defined as one who is never *unknowingly* rude. Guy is clearly a gentleman.

'So you *do* have a problem. The library ceiling?' Amy's nod is fleeting but concise. 'Come on, Guy. We're not the enemy. I'm a practical woman.'

For someone so arty, Amy can be single-minded on occasion. Her concentration narrows to a sharp point. She steps forward, and Guy, intimidated by her statuesque authority, totters back from the doorway. We take this as an invitation, cross the tiny inner hall and walk directly into the library.

It's a breathtaking room, the essence of what this house once was. Elegant, extending the full depth of the left wing, with tall windows on three sides, gold-lacquered pier tables between, and floor-to-ceiling bookcases everywhere else. There's a vast stone fireplace, and above, a coat of arms, the carving picked out with blue, rose, and gold leaf. The Loughnian coat of arms, an airy confection of feathers and roses. The design wouldn't look well on a shield going into battle.

22

No swords or rampant animals. Fortunately battles with shields were over by the philosopher's time. A domed clock here, a lady's sewing-box there, classical vases. It's as if a moment of the eighteenth century is frozen here. A writing-table under one of the windows is piled high with books and an accumulation of closely-written A4. Guy has been at work. The intellectual life of the eighteenth century continues.

So it would seem. But the room is lit against the grey afternoon by two lamps in the far corner. You'd expect them to form a warm circle of light, as in Amy's room, suggesting buttered toast in the offing, but the bulbs are too stingy and the light only adds a new dimension of gloom. Rusty black firedogs languish in the hearth, cold from a draught coming down the chimney. A cheap one-bar electric fire directs pale, thin-blooded warmth towards Guy's desk. But, more seriously, one corner of the ornate plaster panelled ceiling has a blotch of tannin-coloured infection. Like a scar on the face of a beautiful woman. It's obscene. Below stands a misshapen aluminium bucket, resonant with the steady plop of water.

'My God,' says Adelaide with layers of sympathy. The tea-brown stain seems to edge further forward by the second as we watch. 'Should we get a ladder or something? Amy?'

'It's your roof tiles,' says Amy. 'What have you done about it?'

'I've ordered a man,' says Guy. 'One who claims acquaintance with the needs of a roof. Though he happens to be a plumber.'

'Poor Guy,' says Grace. 'Your lovely ceiling.'

'It'll dry out,' says Guy. 'Now that you've had time to gloat, perhaps you would kindly leave. Allow me to proceed with my work.'

'You know what men are like,' says Amy. 'Take

hours to get anywhere. We should put the bucket at source, and stop more damage to the ceiling.'

'Amy's got brains,' Adelaide admits. She's of a practical mind herself, though not active with it. She points to the bucket. 'We must go up to your bedroom.'

Guy stares despairingly around him. 'I store tables and chairs up there. Furniture from the rooms I'm forced to rent out to you.'

'You should put that in the cellars,' says Adelaide.

'The cellars are damp.'

'Where do you sleep, Guy?' By the look on her face, Grace has already guessed.

'Dear people,' says Guy, abruptly deciding to charm us. A glimmer of how he might have looked as a youth shadow-dances across his face. He can make his eyes twinkle at will, like cold stars. 'I can take up no more of your precious time.' He holds the door open invitingly, and with a commanding smile.

'But where do you sleep, Guy?' Adelaide latches on to the implications in Grace's question.

'I have a room below,' says Guy, gathering his dignity about him. 'Perfectly adequately ventilated.'

The telephone rings on his desk. 'Yes?' His face drops. 'Typical British workmen,' he snarls. 'No wonder Brussels is winning the war. I suppose you're taking a further week off to get over New Year? Why not add another day to buy Easter eggs?' He puts the phone down. 'Some misshapen lager lout has gone sick with paternity leave and so the plonking plumber can't get to me before Christmas. He's bloody Welsh, so what can you expect?'

'The Welsh are a cunning lot,' says Amy. 'I wouldn't put money on a Welshman.'

'*We're* here,' says Adelaide. She's a mix between Amazon warrior and Latin matriarch. The opposing qualities cancel each other out.

'If he doesn't get it done, what further damage might occur? I can only just afford this.'

'You've got the money from the Street-Langtons. You said they paid rent up front, a year in advance,' Adelaide points out. 'You haven't drunk it, have you?'

'It paid off the cost of previous repairs. The bank got stroppy. Talked about debt. Never been in debt in my life. Debt means drink and gambling. I just borrow their money at exorbitant rates. A gentlemen's agreement it should have been, if that man hadn't risen out of primeval slime. Bank managers and plumbers, all out of the same trough.'

Amy substitutes the bucket with a Wedgwood vase, the blue and white variety whose touch sets the teeth on edge. Now a different musical note sounds as the water plops down. She empties the bucket through the window, raises her free arm briefly, and says, 'Lead me to your leak.'

Guy, overcome by the presence of determined women, reluctantly takes us up what had been the back stairs, which lead off his vestibule hall. I'm keen to evaluate his living arrangements. The pre-war linoleum on the stairs is of a watery orange design, softened by the years to a pale and greasy apricot, no more attractive for that. Once the servants had silently trod these stairs, all but invisible as they served their masters.

There are three doors at the top of the first flight, and a blocked-off passage that must lead to the rest of the first floor, which is Grace and Adelaide's apartment. Adelaide opens a door, into a room with drawn curtains. Piled high are chairs, sofas, beds, side-tables, serving-tables, crates of china, boxes of clothes, chests, mirrors, pictures of dead animals, and many books. There's a huge mahogany dining-table with six legs, and a pervading smell of mothballs. The ceiling drips water in one corner, water on its way to the library.

'Up further,' decides Amy, heaving the bucket along. 'To the attics.'

In the corresponding room above, a servant's bedroom of smaller dimensions, the plaster has come down. Paper hangs like a thirsty man's tongue, wagging benignly as water splashes onto it. In this dusty room, breathing yesterday's air, we stare in silence. Except it isn't silence. There's no sound other than the water, yet I feel someone is weeping. I glance at Grace, the most likely candidate, but she stands tearless, with her hands pressed together.

Amy scrambles over a Victorian *chaise-longue* and threads her way between tables. She sites the bucket and we hear the plop of rain against metal. 'Don't forget it,' she says to Guy. 'If it overflows, you'll be back where you started.'

Guy sighs, more an upheaval of his lungs than a sigh. No sign of gratitude.

Adelaide's missing. She managed the first flight of stairs OK. I guess what *she's* up to.

We're almost back to the library, when Adelaide calls up from the stairs leading to the cellar. 'I've overshot. Can't see a thing.'

'Well you won't,' Guy shouts back. 'The bulb's gone at the foot of the stairs.'

'I'll put a light on in one of the rooms. To illuminate my way.'

'Bloody woman,' says Guy and goes stumbling down.

We follow him. He tries to wave us back, cross and ineffectual.

He attempts to shove Adelaide back up the stairs but she's a strong woman. The light reveals Guy's bedroom. He sleeps in the original kitchens. Green-glossed walls, light-bulbs without shades, raffia mats, the sort most people use to sunbathe on in Greece.

I've known many inadequate women in my time, most of my family fall into that category, but even such women can attract to themselves a semblance of comforts. They wear shawls and embrace mugs of tea, they push the worst of the dirt out of sight. They hang up unwatered spider plants that refuse to die, they furnish the window-sill with postcards from friends. They proffer enveloping arms and know how to murmur comfort at no cost. Men are not like this.

I stare at the single bed in the corner of the small room, perhaps once the housekeeper's office. There's a high window near the ceiling, with a metal grating outside and a smell of soil. Beyond that is brick wall holding the earth back from the basement. There's one small whitewood chest of drawers and a rail like you get in dress shops, that serves as a wardrobe. There isn't even a chair. Under the bed where the sheets don't reach to the floor are curls of dust, like small field animals sleeping.

I know for certain that Guy, though unmarried, is not gay. He's not sensual enough. He's not creative, he's not spiritual. He has no feminine qualities.

Through a doorway I spot a small cooker. No need to look further. I imagine the few pans, the tins of beans, the chipped sink.

Guy peers round like a startled bat, his once good looks still undiminished by his domestic poverty. Even in adversity his voice is beautifully modulated. 'A simple life,' he says without apology. 'My work is what matters. Have you finished your inspection? Shall we go up?'

Amy, lacking curiosity over Guy's sleeping arrangements, has returned to the library to contemplate the ceiling. She holds up her hands, elbows to her side, in an infinitely brief gesture of benefaction. 'The torrent is ceased,' she says, and a light of satisfaction flickers momentarily in her serene grey eyes.

To the side of the fireplace is a portrait of a man at his writing-desk. Quite young, perhaps about thirty. The rough fabric of his coat, the minimum of lace at the cuff, shows a man not much interested in fashion. The papers and books surrounding him suggest intelligence. Not a large picture, but arresting because of his eyes. They're blue, and so pale. Haunted, sensitive, full of longing. They look how my soul feels in the night.

Guy sees me staring. 'It's a Reynolds. An excellent portrait of Milo Loughnian. Worth something, I can tell you.'

'Your nest-egg,' says Adelaide. 'Something to fall back on. When your roof finally blows away.'

'Good God, woman. Do you honestly think I'd sell that? Milo's the heart of this house. The centre of my own work. Only a bleeding philistine would come out with that remark.'

'Do you know much about him?' I ask, partly to deflect the flak from Adelaide, but mostly because the picture's caught my interest. Those pale blue eyes of the portrait watch me now. Full of a question. Looking as if waiting for an answer. What question do you ask, Milo Loughnian?

'His grandfather built this house, you know, and his father modernized it. It stands on land where there was once an abbey. Fortunately, none of that remains. We stay free from the ghosts of virginal, interfering and pixilated nuns, thank God. Also, I have his journals, which I'm preparing for publication. I'm informed that in their present form they're too unstructured. I continue his scholarship.'

'Milo was the philosopher? What was it he thought?'

'He was fascinated by the nature of goodness. He wasn't an original thinker, of course. He didn't come up with anything new. He was correlating ethical ideas

28

throughout history. Absorbing study. Took the view originally that goodness could be arrived at by reason. Not something you ladies would understand. Reason alone can reveal the true nature of goodness. Unfortunately got a bit deflected by David Hume. I look on the editing of the journals as my life's work.'

No answer to this. If Guy has access to the nature of goodness, how come he's so rude? So mean? Milo, on the other hand, looking at his portrait, seems nothing like Guy. As if he's still searching. I often wonder about goodness myself. Since I've given up God, and my parents never have been reliable guides, and I despise the teachers at school, from where will come the concept good? Does it need to come? It's a shame Guy isn't more like Milo. I'd like to discuss it.

Amy comes over with a benign expression. She's been going round the edges of the bookshelves with a tissue. 'Christmas the day after tomorrow.'

'Bloody purgatory,' Guy bags his forehead against the window-frame. 'Why are we plagued with these domestic trappings?'

Amy holds her arms out wide. An unusual exercise for her. 'I propose we should eat together. In communion.' She stands in the gloom of the afternoon, the rain still tipping down against the window behind her. The table lamp throws its tepid gleam against her left cheek, her splendid nose restricting the light across the rest of her face. I could hug her. Amy's warm and kind, a force for good, and for happiness in this beautiful but miserable room.

'Yes,' says Grace. 'Yes, yes.' Her fingers tremble up to her face.

Guy looks pityingly on us all, his top lip sneaking up the length of his teeth like a horse laughing. He says slowly, with beautiful vowels, 'I can conceive of

29

nothing more *ghastly* than to be cooped up together on the one day everyone deceives themselves they're a happy family.'

'Only for a few hours. We *could* all be happy.' Grace's eyes implore.

'Be happy? Be *happy*? Have you any idea how I can be that?' Guy crumples like a punctured air-cushion and slumps onto an insubstantial chair, face in his hands. 'Money,' he whispers. 'Money, money and more money. I never catch up.' He lifts his face, and his eyes sweep round the room, haunted, frightened. 'This house, this inheritance. My beautiful cursed blessing. It's running away from me.'

Chapter Three

It's perishing cold. Still the rain clacks against the window, like so many Cathies trying to escape the moor.
My bedroom is in a turret, so particularly exposed.
There's no curtain, but the room is too high for anyone
to see in. The turret was a Victorian addition to the
eighteenth-century house, along with the conservatory.
Below is Amy's bedroom, once a morning-room, where
ladies with bustles took a leisurely breakfast, then
wasted away the morning until lunch. The extensions
were tacked on with no attempt to blend the two styles
together, only to increase the living space. Now time
and Amy's décor have melded them together in a manner of their own, echoing Amy's quixotic style.

Under my eyelids, I imagine Guy asleep in the drab,
damp basement, then picture him eating dry toast and
a tinned sausage. I see frustrated Adelaide, and Grace
clinging to the fragile optimism she can't afford to lose.
Amy burying her pain over Henry. This is a sorrowful
place. Everyone's misery comes flooding in to join
with my own, the way drops of rainwater join up on a
window-pane.

For comfort, I imagine Mum is sacked from the pantomime so I can go home. It's not outside the bounds of

possibility, given her talents. In these cold small hours of the night, however, optimism flies away.

There comes the sound of a car driving round the house. Burglars? I get up, curious. There's a lull in the rain. A Lotus Elan whizzes fast round to the back of the house, churning up the mud. The beam from the headlights reveals a shed to the right of the terrace, used as a garage. The car stops with a flash yelp of rubber on the gravel.

Two people get out. When the shed light goes on, I see the man's dark hair grows a long way down his neck, yet sits neatly into his collar without ruffling up. His suit moves like a second skin, tailored to the last centimetre to be part of him. Nothing off the peg here.

She's all long slim skirt with a conker-coloured leather belt. A camel cardigan draped over her shoulders, never in danger of backsliding. No need for a coat as she glides from heated car to warm apartment, expression a natural half-smile. Her hair is a creation, brushed back off her face into a thick wide roll at the back. Victorian but contemporary. I could never do that with mine. There's no way these people are burglars. They must be the Street-Langtons, who can afford a year's rent in advance. She stands perfectly still for a moment in the night air and breathes it in, remembering its scent. They walk in enigmatic silence to a door somewhere below and to the right. Their apartment must be in the Twenties annexe, built to house a new kitchen and maids when the basement was deemed too damp for employees.

I want to hear what these people say to each other. Their conversation will be witty, sophisticated. There's a wonderful lack of the mundane here. I bet they eat Thai takeaways playing a Mozart CD. They are today's equivalent of those who lived here originally. In this sad house, beauty and happiness exist after all, like a

32

pool of light. I'm warmed. I'm defrosted. There's hope for this place yet. They enter their apartment through what must be their kitchen door. They're the most elegant, the most exquisite people I've ever seen in real life. If you are that beautiful, it must be easy to be good.

As the door closes, the man says, 'Get your knickers off, Melissa. I need a seriously inventive fuck.'

I'm doomed to wakefulness. Surely it must nearly be morning. Unable to sleep, I go to the Gothic arched window. Momentarily, the moon illuminates the garden beyond the terrace, and I see Amy standing in the rain, not a stitch on, her arms and her face lifted to the sky. She is stroking her arms as if brushing something off them. I scurry back to bed, putting my head under the bedclothes. Later I hear the door close when Amy returns.

I wake heavy-headed. It's dark still, but the smell of bacon seeps up from below. Today is Christmas Eve. The depressions of the night are fled.

I find Amy in the conservatory. 'Where do I wash?'

'I'll get you a bowl of hot. You can use my room. It might be dangerous going up those stairs too laden.'

'I meant, where's the bathroom?'

'Guy overlooked a bathroom when he carved out this apartment. I've got used to it. Don't quibble any more. There were no bathrooms in the nineteenth century, you know. Not until quite late.'

'Did he forget the loo as well?' I remember that yesterday she *insisted* I inspected the loo off the hall when we returned from seeing Guy. It was quaint. Flowers painted in the bowl. A row of green tiles below a dado.

Amy laughs. This means her lips part slightly and she makes a sort of panting sound, breathy and brief.

'Of course he didn't. We use the one off the main hall. You know where it is.' She flicks her thumb towards the front door.

'*Outside* the flat?'

Amy looks hurt. 'But *inside* the house, Charis. You don't have to go to a shed at the end of the garden, you know.'

I hang on until I've washed. I'm not ready to meet neighbours in my nightdress, especially not the *beautiful* people. I wash in a bowl of water on the pine Victorian washstand. I should have liked to pour the water from a jug, but this is missing.

Amy's kitchen's incorporated into the conservatory. The sink and fridge are cunningly concealed behind a screen of plants. Leggy abutilons waving tangerine bells among ferns, and a Christmas cactus exuberant with flowers like cyanosed shrimps disguise the practical elements, with which Amy feels little empathy.

A claret-coloured Aga warms the room of glass. The cost of the cooker was part of the divorce settlement. Whether it's gleaming clean because Amy is fastidious in the kitchen, or because she doesn't use it much, is hard to say. Mother said at the time she'd made a wise exchange, because Henry is a cold and frugal man, wasted on Amy's plenitude. She puts a kettle on the hotplate.

I listen to it hum into life, hissing gently, a delicate snore. When Henry paid for the Aga, he also paid for the installation, which is ornate. Amy found Victorian tiles, some with pale pink convulvulus and dark green leaves, others with blue poppies amid ochre denticulated foliage. They line the alcove around the cooker, and are old enough to have known the ladies in bustles. On the wall is a sepia photograph of a family in a garden reclining on wicker chairs, with badminton

34

rackets, sailor hats and all the other requirements of a Victorian family afternoon. A family to go with the tiles.

'Who are they?'

'No idea. Found it when I was cleaning out the room you're in.'

'Victorian Loughnians perhaps? Little Milos.'

'I don't think Milo married. Believe Guy said the younger brother took over the house, and *he* was Guy's ancestor.' Amy makes a slight dismissive flick of the wrist. 'They were heavy. The Victorians. Extremely heavy. Their materialism oppresses my soul.'

At the table are chairs with cushions resembling William Morris designs, but actually designed and stitched by Amy. Amongst two-dimensional foliage there lurks a cross-eyed pigeon, and a squirrel with a bandaged paw.

This place has its autonomy, just as Guy's library has, but each of a different age. The difference is that Guy belongs to the room in which he lives. At least, he pretends to, with his reason and his books. Amy does not belong to any time in the past.

'Make the tea then,' says Amy. 'Builders'. Don't go for the perfumed stuff. Henry used to like it. That Fiona woman wooed him with it in the office.'

Eventually we sit companionably crunching bacon and slurping tea.

'Such a funny thing happened this morning.' Amy comes near to giggling, though her mouth retains exactly the same shape as ever. 'I was taking a shower. In the garden. Nothing like natural water for the skin. Just getting the soap off when I saw Guy through the library window. I think he was checking no more tiles were down. He's never up at this time normally. He suddenly looked out of the window and I was forced to adopt the pose of a classical statue. I lingered momentarily, arms aloft. After all, I've got the gravitas. I'm not skinny. When he moved to turn out the light in order to see better, I made off in the dark.'

'He must have recognized you.'

'His mind is above sex, you know. He'd immediately think porcelain nymph or stone goddess.'

The latter more likely.

'You know,' says Amy. 'I can't bear to think of Guy being alone at Christmas. He was so negative about it yesterday.' A flicker of light passes across her eyes. I hear an idea ticking 'We should make one more assault on him. Grace was quite excited by the idea, too. Fortunately I have yet to deliver my Yule cards. That is, tokens assiduously avoiding angels, madonnas, Santas or sheep. I created them in September in a depressed period. They're ready in the studio. We'll deliver them this morning. Casually, but with purpose.'

Her studio lies through a thicket of rhododendrons and azaleas, beyond an archway cut in a wall of yew, on the opposite side of the house to Guy's library. Windows from the Street-Langtons' apartment look over a paved courtyard, and above that a window belonging to Grace and Adelaide. It's the area of stables and outhouses. Through my thin soles, the original cobbles stab my feet as we cross to a tongue-and-grooved door, painted a washed-out grapefruit. The studio was the tack-room of the stable block. At right angles are three stalls, their dark wood partitions decorated with finials of carved feathers, emblem of the Loughnian crest. I momentarily sense the fled smell of horse and of straw, rancid but warm, almost hear the clop of an impatient hoof.

In the north wall of the studio is a huge window, looking out over the drive to the front of the house. It throws a clear, shadowless light into the whole room.

There's a seductive smell of oil paint, warm and rich. Linseed oil and turpentine.

'Guy allowed me to put that glass in,' says Amy. 'I think we should have had planning permission, it's all wrong for the house, but he's scathing about the council. I had to pay for it myself, of course. Well, Henry did. I love it here.'

The first paintings Amy did, after Henry left and she moved to the apartment, were cosy interiors, a lament for lost and warmer days. She sent me one for my birthday. Later she moved to surface design. Her inspiration was William Morris. Like him she spurned the commercial. Her 'Clear Water' phase evolved. Watercolours of sparse flowers, their beauty revealed in the pattern of stems in glass vases, in the relationship of aqua with lime, lavender with khaki, lemon with pale corn. These were the first paintings she sold through a Bond Street gallery.

Two months later she came to the end of that piece of string and moved on to her rustic period with hessian textures and primary oils. The gallery lost interest. The colours would fight with the clients' curtains.

A change comes over Amy as she muses among her canvases in the clear light. She loses the tangible physical presence of the Victorian conservatory, where she was among her possessions. Here, she becomes dissociated from the material, abstracted, and I sense the obscure persona of an artist, existing in creation, in an intangible world, unencumbered by her furniture. She still looks *fairly* hefty.

She surfaces back to reality, picking up cards and envelopes from a table.

'These are my Yule cards. I'm not displeased.' She stares at them, a flicker of a smile threatening to shift her mouth. There are leaping flames, heaving trees, patterns of cinnamon sticks with dried fruits, smiling and winking suns. Not everyone's taste, but *I* like them because they have energy, a life of their own.

'Adelaide and Grace first,' she decides.

Adelaide says 'I never like to drink alone,' so we take the opportunity to knock back a bit of her sherry, and Grace's savoury shortbread biscuits. Here, in their apartment, we're safely back in the past, none of the slightly disorientating shifts of architectural time you get with Amy. This apartment is all eighteenth century, windows and size in agreement. It would have been an impressive bedroom once. Striped brocade curtains, two matching sofas, a real fire which is Grace's responsibility now keep faith with the spirit of the room. Grace constantly punctures the black nuggets with the poker, nudging them to flaunt brighter flames.

The two old ducks agree easily to Amy's plan for a communal Christmas. Grace alternately clasps her hands together and hugs herself. 'I'll pick some mistle-toe,' Adelaide offers. 'Or get Cob to do it.'

Come mid morning, the grape has exerted its influence. We move on to Guy, not waiting to be invited in, knowing Guy's hospitality. We pile in when he opens the door. I try to avoid looking at the ceiling, but it draws my eyes. The brown patch is a deeper shade. It has a permanent look to it.

Guy returns immediately to his desk, reading notes, as if we're not here. Amy, Grace and Adelaide feel the need to brush some of the dust off his belongings, and wander round running a finger over window-sills and chair-backs. It seems only polite to engage Guy in conversation.

'You're always working when we come here.'

Guy's sour face changes. He comes near to a smile. 'My work on Milo goes rather well today. My ancestor, you know. Milo Loughnian. The philosopher. Born 1721. I'm directly descended from his brother.' He seems to have forgotten we had most of this conversation yesterday.

'Milo never published. Pure Enlightenment man. As, indeed, I am. Took as his subject man's concept of good. From Socrates to his contemporaries. He questioned matters such as *Is good innate? Does it come from God? Do you have to reason it out? Is goodness what makes people happy?* He saw his mission as pulling together a complete system of ethical philosophy, once and for all.' Guy's alight now, transported with bloodless enthusiasm.

'Socrates, for example, like many early thinkers, associated good with happiness. He says he who knows what is good, will do good. Because being good will make him happy. Now there's a controversial speculation.'

I'm prepared to chip in here, and point out that since being good often means being unselfish, it doesn't necessarily mean being happy. Like sacrificing your life to look after an aged parent. But Guy is in full torrent.

'Aristotle went further. Decided you could be happy in three ways. Through pleasure. Through being a responsible citizen. Or by being a philosopher.'

'Was Milo happy?' I glance at those pale eyes in the portrait, and cannot think that he was.

Guy doesn't hear me. 'My personal idol is John Locke. Late sixteenth century. That's him.' He hands me a paperweight on his desk. Guy's hero has a miserable, long, thin face with deep eyelids. 'An empiricist. Accepted only what he could see with his eyes. Believed in common sense. Reason tells you how to behave, but that's always as a Christian. Was a democratic, but he didn't want the labouring classes jumped up.'

Guy suddenly shuts up, as if he's divulged too much, shared knowledge only he should have. He gathers the papers to him, covering them with today's *Times*. I'm reminded of Rebecca Winthrop, who does her homework with her arm round what she is writing, so no-one can copy it. I'm never certain whether that's because her work is superior or lousy. Anyway, Guy becomes secretive about what he's writing, just like Rebecca.

Guy shrugs. 'Only *dribbles* left to come, the ones with their Marxist ideas. Feminism hadn't reared its ugly head. No Freud and his obsession with sex. I may add a codicil on that lot. My work is to make Milo's work accessible. If I can do that, my years at Oxford will not have been wasted after all.'

'Is it going well?'

'So so. I'm considering putting a little more emphasis on Locke than Milo chose to do. A man for our time. Common sense, with a bit of religion thrown in. Could do with more of that sort of thing today. Keep the scum down.'

'A truly enlightened man. Just like you, Guy.' The sarcastic voice comes from behind us.

'Less lip from you,' says Guy.

A boy about my age is rummaging through the book shelves. I didn't notice him when I came in. He's short, but thin, not stocky. Every plane of his faces makes angles, like origami. Eyebrows winged, sharp as seagulls. Patches of ginger hair grow against nature. He reminds me of a leprechaun, alien and cheeky, but unreadable. I remember Grace saying she was sure he was a *kind* boy. I understand now the doubt in her voice. Even at this first sight, I sense there is a desire for him to lash out, to wound. Indiscriminately.

I feel myself colouring up, and I can't think why. He'll be nothing to me.

'Can I borrow this book on Hume?' His voice is offhand, uncaring, lacking optimism. He stares directly at me, but speaks to Guy. I turn away, not wanting him to see I'm blushing in this stupid way. I can hardly explain this is what always happens, because I'm so hopeless with boys.

'Try the public lending library.' Guy blows his nose and examines the subsequent contents of his handkerchief with interest.

'They haven't got anything.' The boy's hand still hovers over the book.

'The library van comes to the village every Wednesday.' Guy returns his noserag to his pocket with reluctance.

'Guy, that's all big print and children's stuff.'

Guy stares at the book as if willing it back on the shelf. He doesn't waver.

'Suit yourself.' The boy slouches out of the door, his eyes sliding scornfully over my face again, no doubt noting the pudding shape, straight hair, understated mouth, pale eyelashes.

I'm rather pleased. He's noticed me. I'm generally invisible.

'Goodbye Cob, dear,' calls Grace, pocketing the tissue she's been using as a duster.

So that's Cob who lives in the yard. Obviously a clever stick. Doesn't like Guy. As with many things that disconcert me, he exerts a fascination. 'Who *is* he exactly?'

'An orphan,' says Grace, 'but very self-sufficient.'

'He's damned lucky Guy provides him with a home,' says Adelaide. 'He's got it made.'

'He *is* a relative. His mother was descended from the Loughnian family. Many cousins apart of course. Even if she wasn't dead,' Grace adds. She looks down at her hands, as if her words are a futile but relevant murmur

41

in a storm. I'm not too sure there isn't something she's thinking but won't say.

'A remarkably *distant* relative. *So* distant it's never been spelled out. Far too many second cousins and aunts by marriage to qualify as a relative, to my mind. Guy is under no obligation.' Adelaide clamps her mouth shut as if it's on a spring, and we can see that's the end of that.

I wonder why he doesn't live in the main house. In the yard presumably means in the tiny cottage next to the stables. Why does Guy give him a home at all, when he seems to dislike him so much?

Guy rambles on. 'Can't think what Cob wants with a book on Hume.' He shrugs his shoulders. 'What a prig that boy can be. Got ideas above his station. Apparently trying for a place at university. Says he'll study philosophy. Be quite beyond him, of course. I suppose he's come under the influence of great minds living in the environs of this house. Last book he needs is one about *Hume's* ideas. A heretic to clear thinking, that man.'

'But Milo admired him,' I point out. 'You said he was deflected by him.'

'Milo gave Hume too much credence. Hume, being a heathen, had no recourse to a higher intelligence. So his reasoning was flawed. Worse still, when he contemplated personal morality he forsook philosophy entirely, and rabbited on about a generous heart.'

Guy seems to be mixing up *revealed* ethics with reason here, but I know he won't listen if I try to argue with him.

'Hume did a great deal of damage, undermining established thinking. But what can you expect? The man was a ruddy atheist.'

Grace, still concerned with something in her head, says vaguely, 'Hume fathered a child. A village girl.

Don't you remember, Guy? You lent me one of your books.'

'What the hell was I doing, lending *you* a philosophy book?'

'In a mellow moment. More a potted biography, it was. After I expressed a desire to understand your work.'

'That's all you can remember about the man? Not his ideas. Not his work. Only the gossip about a meaningless fling. Typical female. That girl, Agnes, was no better than a hussy. She made up the story. Pregnant serving-wench. Was anybody's. Never proven that Hume was remotely involved.'

Guy seem to be contradicting himself again.

'Good feminist attitude you have,' says Amy, sarcasm not even hinted by her face.

'David Hume was a gentleman. Even if it were true, such a dalliance would be of no importance to him.'

I wonder why Guy is protecting him in this way when he rates him so poorly as a philosopher, and a bad influence on Milo.

'If you say so, Guy.' Grace looks quite vacant sometimes.

'What are you doing for Christmas, Guy?' Adelaide asks, not interested in dead men.

'Same as usual. I've already purchased a tin of chicken supreme.'

'We invite you to a simple but exquisite luncheon,' says Adelaide. 'Perhaps an elegant little duck and cranberry confit? A soupçon of sage mousse? My range is endless.' This is not quite what Amy has in mind, but my aunt appears willing to compromise in the interest of togetherness.

'Don't make me do too many fussy bits,' says Grace, meaning no malice, and slaps her hand over her mouth when Adelaide gives her a look.

43

'Duck's disgustingly fatty,' says Guy.

'We'll agree later on a species of bird,' says Amy. 'It's ridiculous for each apartment to be eating a variety of small poultry because we're not enough for a turkey. Think of this house, Guy, in its heyday. Extravagant feasting. Course after course. Servants everywhere. Best silver. Blazing fires. Dancing. Perhaps not dancing this year,' she adds quickly, catching his expression. 'Imagine the house come alive. Vibrant. Full of joy. *You* can make it happen, Guy. *We* can make it happen. This house is crying out for animation and laughter.' Amy leans against the wall, exhausted. She's put her vision before us. 'Why *can't* we have one big Christmas dinner together?'

I notice she keeps well away from any mention of Yule now. Neither fire festivals nor the winter solstice feature this morning.

'Let's do that. Oh, let's.' Grace holds her hands together, almost as if in prayer, a supplication to Guy. She giggles inwardly, like a small tumbling brook. 'It'll be cheaper too.'

'We'll keep it quiet compared with the old days.' Amy is soothing. 'Then the rooms would have been interlinked. A room for cards, one for dancing, another for supper.'

'Dancing?' Grace whispers, having missed this the first time.

'Can't do any of that. The doors long since been blocked up. There's a bookcase in the library where there used to be a door to Amy's drawing-room. So *that's* out.' The downward grooves on Guy's face lengthen.

'Luckily we haven't already invested in a bird,' says Adelaide. 'We go to the market in Stevenage quite late, and purchase a reduced remnant.'

'We can't do it,' says Guy, grasping for an excuse.

'You can't replicate the past. Besides, the Street-Langtons have the original dining-room.'

The Street-Langtons. The *beautiful* people.

'They're invited as well.' Amy makes an uncharacteristically wide sweep of her arms to show the inclusive, all-enveloping nature of the project. 'Then perhaps they'll oblige.'

'They're going to the Seychelles.' Guy smirks, relieved. 'Thank God for that. What an upheaval it would all have been.'

'I saw Anthony in the hall this morning. The good news for us is,' says Grace, words spilling over, 'their travel company's gone bust. I'm sorry to say he blasphemed. Elegantly, of course. But not nice words. They're staying put until the New Year.'

'The fates are with us. What about it then, Guy?' Amy asks.

Guy sighs heavily and elaborately. His shoulders sink like melting ice-cream sliding down a cone. Amy's prevailed. 'If we must,' he says, and searches for his handkerchief again.

'We'll each bring one present,' says Amy, her mind leaping ahead. 'Something suitable for anyone. Guy, you can distribute them after the meal. Give you something to do.'

'I won't get anything appropriate,' says Guy. 'Probably tights, or a vase. I won the raffle at the church garden party last summer. A knitted rabbit. Holding a knitted carrot.'

Grace has a list, crumpled now from clutching it to her flat chest. As we cross the hall she shyly catches my arm. 'Charis, would you be sweet and find Cob. He might do these errands for me.'

'Are you inviting Cob to Christmas dinner?' How stupid I am. I've alerted them to his presence. I only wanted to be certain he *wouldn't* be there, that his

45

goblin presence won't hover menacingly over Christmas Day. That I wouldn't suffer his scornful stare.

'Of course,' says Grace. 'He's got nowhere to go. Ask him for us, dear, when you give him the list. Nice for you, Charis, to have another young person. He may be in the Italian garden.'

Chapter Four

Because the proper education for an eighteenth-century young man was visiting Renaissance cities on the Grand Tour, many English gardens subsequently took on the classical influence. Country-house designers were required to lay out their gardens as separate landscapes, like rooms through which to walk. The garden became an extension of the house. To the left of Loughnian House, on the library side, is just such a garden, small, wall-protected, complete in itself.

The Italian garden shows its classical ancestry, with a rectangular ornamental pool and Roman villa-style summer-house. The narrow columns support a porch over the stoa, hoping to give the impression that Roman thinkers still pace about in its shade, arguing in Latin. Stoicism, the resulting philosophy, claims that good lies within the state of the soul. Therefore the Romans created peaceful gardens to influence the harmony of the soul. Unfortunately, this enthusiasm for philosophical virtue was not reflected in their *political* history.

Perhaps Milo Loughnian designed and created our Italian garden himself, this oasis of calm. Possibly he sat here of an evening, contemplating virtue. Perhaps stoic tranquillity prevailed here then. Today there is neither peace nor order. Tall reeds under the hedges are dank and rotting. Medieval sorrow is the essence of this house. *The sedge is withered from the lake and no birds sing.* More Gothic than Roman. Why is Loughnian House so sad?

'*O what can ail thee, knight-at-arms?*' I whisper, overwhelmed with sadness, with a frustration that doesn't come from within myself.

From the beech tree in the corner hang a few remaining bronze leaves, so tentatively that they lose grip and flutter down from time to time. I catch one and inspect it, observe its veins, its warm colour. For each falling leaf you catch, you have one happy day in the next year. I don't attempt to catch any more leaves. One happy day is all I could possibly hope for. I press the leaf against my forehead and let its promise seep into my brain.

'Looking for me?' Embarrassed, I turn, recognizing that scornful voice.

Cob emerges from the summer-house with a piece of sacking. He leans against the pillar, mocking. How long has he been watching me mutter and catch leaves? His pale blue eyes are expressionless, but disconcerting. Cheekbones like a sparrow's wing, angular and unfleshed. His mouth droops as if he's tired. He's fractionally less menacing outdoors. Perhaps because Guy isn't around.

I don't know what to do next, whether to stand my ground, or walk away with some shred of dignity. Walking away is to admit defeat, and anyway I don't feel dignified. What's the matter with me? I'm socially dysfunctional. By the time I remember the messages, Cob gives up on me, and starts cutting holly from the hedge. He puts it down on the sacking. I can smell the hessian, its dry-soil mustiness, dusty and unpleasant.

He hums loudly to himself while he works, as if I'm not there. I think it's 'The Hebrew Slaves' Chorus'. *Nabucco*. Eventually he says, 'Grace likes to decorate their rooms.' He almost smiles, a fleeting quirk.

'She wants you to have this list.'

'Got a list from her already.'

'These are additions. We're having Christmas dinner together. All of us. I've been told to invite you.' So eager to hide my embarrassment at having to invite him, I'm cold and offhand.

'Tell them I'll think about it.' He stops hacking at the holly. 'Might be worth it just to spoil Guy's day.' The eyebrows scoot upwards, like an imp.

'Guy was mean over the book.'

'I'll be doing philosophy at university next year. He doesn't like that.'

'Why not?'

'I'll get a degree, won't I?'

'Guy went to Oxford.'

'He *went* to Oxford but he didn't get a degree. Just messed about. Then left. It bothers him no end. Are *you* having turkey with the masses?'

'No choice. Why philosophy?' The subject would never have occurred to me.

He stares into the distance, as if I'm not here. 'The ability to think clearly gives you power. Words give you power. The sort of power that counts even more than money.' Cob doesn't scare me now. I see what drives him. He's fighting because he's poor. Vulnerable. Envious. This conversation is real, not like at school, when all talk centres on clothes, the top ten and boys. I think I could almost talk to Cob about goodness, whereas I never would be able to with Guy.

He almost smiles, just one side of his mouth. 'Got my driving licence last week. Taking the van to the supermarket this afternoon.' There's pride in his voice.

'Want to come?' His look isn't inviting. He's as offhand as me.

'No thanks.' He only asks to show off. Because there's no-one here to invite.

'Suit yourself.'

Already I regret refusing. It would have been something to do. I shouldn't be stupid, he's not interested in me. That's for sure. And I'm not interested in him.

Amy comes from Guy's apartment, hunting for her front-door key, rifling through her bag like her arm's down a drain. She searches its depths, face averted. Grace and Adelaide totter upstairs.

Anthony Street-Langton strides out of his door off the hall, in a Barbour jacket, and cap tipped well forward. A certain key to class is the angle at which a man wears his cap, and how his hair juts out beneath, at the back. An infallible guide. Melissa follows, in a heavy riding-coat, casual over camel leg warmers and loosely belted black sweater reaching mid thigh. You usually only see clothes flung on like that in *Vogue* magazine, carefully posed and still. She can actually move around, and they still look good. She smiles at us, showing her lovely teeth, as she glides across the hall. The friendly waggle of her fingers seems out of character.

'So many lovely ladies,' says Anthony, and kisses each of us on the cheek, grasping the shoulders with warm, confident hands. I can smell the man smell of him. Alive. Forceful. He runs up the stairs two at a time to kiss Grace and Adelaide. 'Mmm. Mmm. Mmm,' he says. 'Everyone ready for the big day?'

I almost forget Anthony's crude comments in the overheard conversation last night. The Street-Langtons' sex life is another and unknown article of their glamour. It's not something I should speculate about, what girls at school call the *Ultimate Experience*. Another enlightenment denied to me, like wearing cashmere.

'Just the people I want to see,' coos Adelaide. 'Would you care to join us all for Christmas dinner? A joint project. Bring Loughnian House alive again. A *traditional* Christmas.'

'What do you think, darling?' Anthony raises one quizzical eyebrow, teasing and attractive.

'Lovely,' says Melissa. She doesn't sound at all upset at the prospect of slumming with us.

'At *our* place, do,' says Anthony, and holds up his hands like a conjuror. A cheeky vivacious conjuror, who has more than rabbits in his hat. 'We have the original dining-room. Keep it trad. Got the Harrods number, darling? Food-hall extension?'

'Only the turkey is missing,' says Grace. 'I've done the baking.'

'I'll get something a bit special,' says Anthony. ' *Sans* feathers.'

Melissa says, 'We could do with a bigger table.'

'Guy has one, dear,' says Adelaide, and flourishes her hand vaguely as if that is sufficient to move it. 'In the attic. Saw it only yesterday.'

Guy, Cob and Anthony make a terrible fuss bringing the table down. Anthony lies flat on the top landing and lets it slide down the stairs. 'Like it's on skis,' he calls. 'Reminds me of Davos. Did the steepest run on the Parsenne at midnight. With torches. Like comets whistling down the mountain. Pretty exhilarating. Blind drunk at the time, of course.' Cob and Guy, unimpressed, wait at the bottom.

This could be the table Milo used. I shall remember him tomorrow, almost as if he's coming himself to join us. It's solid mahogany, oval-shaped when the drop

51

leaves lift up. The six pad-shaped feet resemble those of some gentle animal. Such a patina of polish built up over the years it's rewarding just to buff and see the gleam coming back. We put the chairs that go with it, with their violin-shaped splats, around the table. The table is in its rightful room. This is a plank towards remaking the house as it should be.

Perhaps Amy's concept of the commune is bringing the whole house together, not just the people living here now. The house needs all its parts, the reason of Milo, the romance of the William Morris Victorians, perhaps it needs servants and children as well. These people are gauze-fine ghosts under my eyelids. What would it take to summon them into the room?

'Wonderful,' breathes Amy. 'Each playing their part in the greater whole. A microcosm of life. Should I draw up some House rules, do you think?'

'You bloody won't,' says Guy. 'Too many gabbling women telling me what to do already.'

'Get a bit of holly in for us, there's a good man,' Anthony tells Cob.

'Right, sir,' says Cob with mock deference, and slouches out, back to the Italian garden. Looks as if Anthony is someone else Cob doesn't like.

'Weird person,' says Anthony while admiring the shine on his nut-brown polo boots. His feet are quite small. 'Say, Charis. You're doing a great job there.' He sits on the window-sill and gives me this gorgeous grin showing off all his lovely teeth. They're dead even and so white. No-one is born with teeth that perfect. Except possibly Americans. These are teeth with attitude. They must have cost.

'Which one is it?' Guy mutters, giving each chair a shake. He's determined to find something wrong. He doesn't want joy. ' There's one that's broken. Yes. That one over there. Been repaired at some time. Still a bit rickety. Whoever gets that better watch it.'

Melissa has changed into a long skinny knitted suit in soft coral wool. With her hair casually tied back with a piece of braid the same colour, she looks like a model with nothing much to do but drape gracefully. She runs her fingers over the repaired back. 'How did that happen?' Melissa laughs. 'Some weight to break that.'

'You'd never do it then, dear,' says Grace.

Melissa smiles in her dreamy way. 'Can I help with the cooking, tomorrow?' There's a hint of animation ruffling her calm voice, and I'm not certain whether it's anxiety or excitement.

'Grace cooks *wonderfully*,' says Amy, who doesn't notice the subtext in the tone.

'My Gran always did goose for Christmas. Two of them for all our family. My Gran loved her goose.'

Anthony says, 'Do you really mean *my Gran*, darling? Why not be fractionally wittier? Grandee, or GB for Granny Brenda. Something with a bit more style. *Something*. You're not quite up there with your gorgeous image.'

'My Gran is my Gran,' says Melissa, with the stubbornness that usually only comes from the downtrodden.

'Suit yourself.' Anthony goes out to his flashy sports car to purchase our communal Christmas bird. He's changed as well. These people have a fantastic amount of clothes. He's wearing very loose casual trousers and a shirt with a grandad neck. His hair is at that wonderful point before it needs a cut, of full volume flopping onto his forehead and nestling into the nape of his neck. It's very shiny and clean. 'Better get in some liquors. We don't want to be caught out with elderberry wine.' He addresses Guy and walks past Melissa without speaking to her. Could they be having a row? I'm totally at sea how beautiful people behave. Naïvely, I expect perfection. If you're beautiful everything must be so easy. It's strange he doesn't speak *to* her. He speaks *at* her, treating her like a child, telling her how to behave.

'What about crackers?'

'Crackers? For God's sake, Melissa. Can you see *me* in a paper hat?'

Amy gives an unexpected wink. She's breathy with pleasure. *I'm* wondering who'll ruin this Christmas. Cob? Guy? Even the gorgeous Anthony slipping off his pedestal.

Amy, her hair quivering with energy, whispers, 'I really think the commune is beginning to gel.'

Chapter Five

We go to Midnight Mass, which Amy and I shouldn't do. It's wrong to act religious if you're not. I don't believe in anything, but I'm going out of manners, because the others will frown on Amy if we behave like heathens. Amy shouldn't be going either. She has no God, only pagan forces, but *she* goes for the sake of the Commune. If she doesn't move with them, she can't expect them to move with her. We all walk down to the village at the same time, not because this is a dangerous area, but Amy herds us together. Cob isn't with us. I'm not surprised. He's true to himself, not a hypocrite like me.

I get a bit ahead, because I'd like to find Milo Loughnian's grave. I'm wondering how his friends and family remembered him. What caring words did they engrave on his headstone? I have a torch and spot the headstone easily, because it's at the edge of the graveyard to the west. It's stark and simple. Too simple.

Milo Loughnian

Born 1721. Died 1759.

That's all. No kind words. No loving memory. Only cold, loveless facts.

Guy catches up with me. His voice is muffled, because the Paisley scarf wrapped round his neck encroaches on his face, like an eggcup supporting an egg. 'I sometimes wonder,' he says, 'if that's the original grave. I would have expected some small tribute to his genius. At the end of last century the burial ground was extended to the south and to the west. Which seems odd, as Milo is buried right on the western boundary. There was no record of reburials. I often wonder, you know.'

We go into the church, which is small, dark with candlelight, and smelling of wet floorcloth, damp hymn-books and spent candle-wicks. Some might mistake it for an aura of holiness. The locals have arrived early, they turn round and stare. Except for Grace, those from the Philosopher's House only go at Christmas. Adelaide trips over a hassock carelessly left lying about, and, to save herself, embraces a pedestal arrangement of holly and plastic Christmas roses. She blasphemes, and not quietly, which gets us off to an endearing start.

We file into two pews near the back, Adelaide leading the way.

'Terrible draught here,' she says. 'We'll move further forward.'

We reverse out into the aisle, shunting like a train. Unfortunately the choir has already started to process from the back. We cut them off from the vicar, which soon wipes the benign Christmas smile off his face. By the time we've shunted further forward, into a less draughty spot, there's so much clucking from the front you'd think a fox was among the hens. I sense more hostility from them than goodwill. Amy aggressively grasps her black wool shawl, hugging it to her against the cold. She is detached, distant, not a part of this place.

In front of us sit Melissa, Anthony and Grace. Melissa's chestnut army-style coat is of such soft expensive fabric that it hangs like silk. The ruffled fake-fur collar stirs gently, as if alive, in the cross-eddies of air currents between vestry and door. Dreamily, she stares up at the roof, as if searching for something elusive. Anthony's camel coat is long, the belt tied in a knot although it has a perfectly good buckle. The sort of coat worn by bigamists and con men in pre-war films. He watches every kneel or upstanding of those in front. It's important to Anthony to know what's what before God.

Grace's body language is clear. There's a hood to her best black coat, which suggests the medieval cleric. Most of the time she barely moves, as if reluctant to disturb the holy air. Head cast down even in the hymns, as if the light from her Lord is too bright. When she kneels in prayer, and she's the only one of our lot to get down there on the hassock, she presses herself ardently against the pew in front, agonizing. Every day is Good Friday for Grace.

Beside me, Adelaide eyes up the women in anoraks, and felted coats that aren't the right length, the men in suits which are not their everyday gear. She glances down, approving her own Canadian squirrel three-quarter jacket. She treats the congregation to descant. The choir is deficient in this area, as in most, since it comprises two men long past the day when their pensions were a novelty, one sharp-featured woman, whose angular prow and stiff hair are unlikely companions to harmony, and one precocious child, probably a boy. I'm not musical, despite my gifted family, but I recognize a cacophony when I hear it.

Guy closes his eyes a lot when he sings, but keeps

57

them open in the prayers. During the address he cleans under his fingernails with a penknife.

Amy does nothing, neither sings nor prays. She sits still and calm, the hint of a smile in her elephant-grey eyes, aloof and waiting.

I'm always uncomfortable in churches. They fill me with negative thoughts. If God is perfect, why would he want us to *worship* him? Why do prayers give constant instructions to the One who is all-knowing? Has man created gods in all their variety because he can't accept that man's life is finite? Are we so *egotistic,* so *self-centred* that we refuse to accept we all come to dust?

I bet God hates Christmas. Gets a right ear-bashing at the largest turnout of the year. An extended ear-bashing, because of time zones, though with a lull when midnight falls over Saudi Arabia.

In the event Christmas Day falls into three areas, each quite separate. Later I will remember them distinctly, as if they were never part of the same day. There is a pre-commune period.

I wake, and see the morning star to the east in a clear sky before the dawn. It's bright this morning, as if shining down to protect us all. Venus. Named after the goddess of love. If I believed, I would look up to that star and imagine God was within its pure light.

I watch the sky begin to lighten, and know I'll feel let down by lunch-time. My experience of Christmas is always of being let down. You spend two months working towards the day, culminating in all the expectation created by the rituals of Christmas Eve, then nothing is any different. Something always went wrong at home with dinner. One part wasn't cooked, something else was burned. In the afternoon people dozed, got quarrelsome on account of too much to drink with the turkey. I can't see today being different.

No smell of bacon cooking, which I need to get off to a good start. Trying to feel festive, I go down to Amy's room. She isn't there, but the bed's made. There's not much light coming from the rest of the apartment. I go through the bedroom and into the conservatory.

Then everything's magic. It's still dark outside, with the dawn appearing beyond the trees. A candelabra of five lighted candles stands on the table, their flames reflected and multiplied in the windows all around. A festival of lights. The CD plays the 'Siegfried Idyll'. Wagner again, but this time softly. Not like the 'Walküre', which needs to blast out. Amy leans back against the conservatory door, warming her hands round a mug of coffee, smiling secretly because this she has done for me. She wears a long-sleeved dress of damson flocked wool, which reaches three inches from the floor. I feel her generosity engulfing me, like a hug.

'If you go to my clothes rail, you'll find a velvet tunic. Ilex green. Your colour. You can borrow it if you like. We can look Gothic together.'

Mainly to oblige Amy, I put the tunic on over my jeans. It's about the right size for me, so Amy can't have worn it for years. I surprise myself. Since there's a shortage of mirrors, I look at my reflection in the windows. I'm slinky. Today, nondescript me has acquired something of Amy's aura. This I should use. To this I should attain.

Amy says in a hushed and reverent voice, 'Today the sun is reborn. It's out there over Australia and that, and now it's turning back to us. The candles' flames encourage it.' She levers herself off the door and waltzes round the table. 'And I've got over Henry.'

'Do you think *I* should be a pagan?'

'*I'm* not a pagan. I don't believe in their gods. I'm not a New Ager. I haven't lit the candles because of the solstice fire at all. I've done what people have done since the first days. Creating a bit of light and joy in the deepest cold of the year. People have always done it, but with a variety of excuses. We all need these diversions. Treats to cheer.'

Through the window, in the clearing darkness Grace takes a short cut across the garden. She's been to church again. Not enough for her the noisy hymns of the Midnight Mass, beer on the breath at the communion table, materialism in the heart. Grace would love the Spartan cold of the church in the early morning, breathing in the stale candle smoke, being among the few. God should be grateful he has Grace.

Amy does another quick twirl celebrating her release from loving Henry, before inspecting the turkey's cooking in the slow oven, its smell locked within since eleven o'clock last night. Anthony insisted on buying the bird from Harrods. He rushed out and bought it in the late afternoon. Seventy-mile round trip. I can't think what difference that will make. Harrods didn't *rear* it in the food hall, did they? The smell of turkey fills the conservatory.

We exchange presents. I give Amy a book about Sickert. I bought it for her in Waterstones the day I knew I'd been invited. She's thinking of going impressionist herself quite soon. She gives me some wind chimes wrapped in paper decorated with smiling suns. 'Earth energy converted into music,' she says. I realize every place I live, including home, school and the bedroom upstairs, is so draughty, the damned things will be dinging and donging all night.

Amy cooks eggy breads for breakfast, allegedly white bread in a crisp egg coat. I shouldn't be critical and point out they're limp as wet washing. She didn't get the fat hot enough. Never mind, they go a treat with HP sauce.

We have Mexican coffee, which is with a cinnamon stick. Amy pours in some tequila as well, to make it especially Mexican, though less authentic. We repair to the sitting-room and sit serenely on the striped sofa, amid the strewn wrapping paper. Amy always sits there cross-legged, relaxed yet alert. She's like a Buddha, or a Bodhisattva, one who has glimpsed nirvana. Her tranquillity is infectious, a calm handed on from one candle flame to another, like the breath of life itself. I feel stronger for being near her, at the calm in the eye of the storm that is Amy's lifestyle. Or it could be the tequila.

'The *Mexicans* were very pagan,' she says. Amy spent ten days in Mexico in the spring to get over Henry. Apparently it hadn't worked. She says, 'Their gods, Chaac and Chac-mool, and Pacal the priest-king, remind me of Henry quite painfully. *They* were all sex-mad, you know.'

'I don't understand how he could leave you.' I'm full of sympathy and warmth. 'I bet he's not drinking Mexican coffee and tequila for breakfast with Fiona.'

'Half a grapefruit, and muesli with extra bran on top, I would imagine.'

'Do you think a healthy low fat yoghurt as it's Christmas?'

Amy is bored with breakfast talk. 'I think it must have been the sex,' she muses. 'He liked licking. Everywhere. Under the covers. Like some small burrowing animal. Most *irritating*. He came out from under the duvet one day to find me browsing through the catalogue for the Royal Academy summer exhibition. It was never quite the same since then.'

Mother rings at nine o'clock. 'The merriest of times, my darling,' she cheeps. 'I'd be with you myself, but

I'm at the electrician's house. Did I mention Nick at all? That's where I am.'

'Happy Christmas.'

'The very, very happiest to you. We're going to his mate's for lunch. Nick's mate. I've told you about Nick? We're on the Buck's fizz at the moment. Not had anything to eat yet.' I can tell that.

'Darling are you happy? I so want you to be happy. You do know that don't you?'

'I'm very happy, Mum.'

'Are you sure?'

'I'm sure.'

'Goodbye darling. Big, big kisses.'

I think of my mother, and what other people would call her shortcomings. She may not be very motherly, but I'm comfortable with her. I understand her. She's a moth in the night seeking love. It's an endless quest. And painful. Sometimes I feel very fond of my mother, especially when she's not around.

Chapter Six

The second part of the day is the coming together. We collectively prepare dinner in Melissa's kitchen, with its breakfast bar, high stools, array of stainless steel, ceramic surfaces, ice blue sponge-painted doors. It's as self-consciously modern as the Twenties was when the wing was built. Like Amy, the Street-Langtons have mixed architecture. The original eighteenth-century dining-room plus the modern extension. Anthony and Melissa have unified their apartment by making everything strikingly up to the minute. Anthony style.

I struggle to get up on a stool, but Melissa arrives aloft with an elegant vault. Together we assemble smoked-salmon canapés. Adelaide isn't much help. Instead of her usual Alice headband she has a modified turban coiled through her extra bright auburn hair. You could call her handsome. She doesn't attempt a high stool. She has a two-pound box of chocolates on the kitchen table among the prepared vegetables, working her way through the soft centres. Occasionally she offers us a pick.

Grace is transformed, not only by her enormous white apron, but by culinary enthusiasm. She fantails the roast potatoes, wielding the knife with total disregard for her safety; wraps sausages in bacon like piglets in a blanket, spices the cranberry sauce with cinnamon and orange peel. Her colour-drained skin takes on a damp shine. Anthony gives her a champagne cocktail with so much brandy, it looks as if it's been drunk before. Her cheeks pink up.

Amy picks cloves out of the bread sauce, staring out of the window. She's momentarily distant from us. I hope she's not reverting to Henry.

The meal is timed for four o'clock. Amy suggested this as it would bridge afternoon and evening, and so extend the period of communality. Surprisingly, Guy backed her up, saying that was the time the gentry ate in the eighteenth century, with supper at ten. He quickly added that a second meal would be surplus to requirements, and anyway would mangle his digestive system.

Anthony inspects the dining-table which Melissa says took her an hour to arrange. The high room could be out of *House and Garden*, the burgundy dark paper casting a glow above the cream dado. Once the walls would have been hung with large portraits, but now there's modern art, abstracts, distorted figures, blank areas of colour in steel frames. Melissa has been traditional with the table. Her Gran would have been proud. The white linen could have been the work of maids in starched aprons, the glasses and gold fruit, symbols of an elusive affluence, the work of the mistress of the house. There's a sense of timelessness here that should be the hallmark of this place, but isn't. Anthony fingers the six miniature arrangements of holly and hellebores at intervals down the length of the table. He stands back to assess the centrepiece of gold-sprayed nuts and fruit, heaped in a dish. The table napkins are water-lilies, white with a gold holly leaf tucked into each.

Anthony tosses the gold holly leaves into the fire,

and carries the dish of nuts over to the sideboard. Some of them roll off. He treads on them, and they become gold shards on the carpet, exposing their dull brown nutty souls within. He sees me staring. 'Gold paint is naff,' he explains.

'It's fashionable.' I'm protective of Melissa's effort.

'There's fashion,' says Anthony, 'and there's *style*.' By the way he stands and very slightly lifts one eyebrow, he demonstrates that Anthony has style. Having none of my own, I watch closely, with a view to plagiarism. One thing I've gleaned about style is that it doesn't need to score, it's independent, it stands alone. Today he wears a draped suit but no shirt. Instead, some sort of silk vest underneath. Not the type that'd keep you warm, nor be practical if your work took you much onto a roof, but more by way of being decorative. Glossy chest hair flourishes above it, a sexy hint of nakedness. Two heavy gold wristlets clink above his left hand, and a streak of gel, not quite polished away, holds his hair in careless perfection. Does it count as style when you work so hard to gain an effect?

Anthony grins, his whole face mobile with energy and exuberance. 'Clean lines, Charis. Minimal fuss. It costs, darling. It sure costs. But if you want it, you can get it.' He comes over and shakes me by the shoulders. As if he's trying to shake style into me. 'Smile at me.'

I smile obediently, smelling his musk perfume.

'More. Bigger smile.' He's looking down at me, willing me.

I can't help it. I begin to laugh. He laughs too.

'That's a start.' He backs out of the room and winks. He says, 'Melissa darling, I've slightly changed the table. Sure you'll approve. Grace, you delicious woman, I love what you're doing to those Brussels.'

I'm glad Cob's not here yet. Perhaps he won't turn up.

He does eventually. About three o'clock when I really thought he might have changed his mind. At least he remembers to bring a present.

'Hello,' he says to me, when he's spoken to everyone else first.

'Hi.'

'You look quite nice.'

'Amy lent me the top.'

'It's good. You've got green eyes.'

'They're grey.'

'They're green. Definitely green.'

'Oh.'

In this moment I fall in love. No boy had ever looked at me long enough to notice the colour of my anything. He says my eyes are green. They're not, or at least they weren't. They will be green now. For ever. For eternity. I can't bear to look at him again, in case he sees into my face. Along the tear-ducts into my heart.

'Having lots of fun in the kitchen?' Cob's back to his scornful self.

'It's OK.'

He picks up a handful of nuts, and chews them noisily, still staring at me.

'Where's Guy?' Amy asks. 'He can't have forgotten, can he? Charis, could you fetch him?'

Getting Guy into the dining-room takes some doing. He's still working at his little desk, even though it's Christmas Day.

'You could have a rest today.'

'There's only me who can do it.' He turns the page over so I can't read what he's written. 'You lot can't understand what Milo was doing. I *must* make him accessible. I'm all he has.'

Poor Guy, an old man neglected by time, his importance stripped from him as the authority of his money and property slips away. Frantically hanging onto the only thing that might be important to the family and to the house. He's safe with his *work*. Much safer than mixing with *us*. It's hard for him to breathe the same air as anyone else. Amy's idea of a commune terrifies him. His work will take the rest of his life. I think of Casaubon in *Middlemarch* trying to pin down all mythology, and feel profoundly depressed for Milo Loughnian.

On the other hand, Guy is possibly doing the first genuine work of his life, rather than living off the fat. I smile encouragingly. 'A dark green cover would be impressive when it's finished.' Green is the paramount colour in my life now.

'What a weird little person you are,' he says, and I realize there's a certain amount of respect in his voice. I have visualized for him that he might reach a conclusion.

One disadvantage of dinner being in the late afternoon is that some have had plenty to drink and not much to eat, while others are totally sober and low in blood sugar.

Cob and Guy belong to the second group, Amy and I to the former. That's why, when it's time to eat, we have a bit of a crisis getting the turkey from Amy's Aga to the dining-room. We have only to cross a corner of the hall, but, as I've pointed out before, the carpet is long past its best. Missing threads expose loops of wool lying loose. Amy inadvertently gets her foot under one of these and lurches against the wall, down which she slowly subsides, gallantly holding the turkey aloft. I struggle to keep parallel with her. All is well until she approaches the horizontal, when the weight becomes too much, and we develop a tilt. The bird rolls off onto the carpet. By good fortune the fatty stain coincides almost perfectly with an Eastern pineapple motif. By the time we've loaded it all back onto the plate and scraped off the fluff no-one would guess it hadn't come direct.

'We think you should carve, Guy.' Adelaide simpers.

'Can't you women chop the bloody bird up your-selves?'

'You're head of the household,' explains Grace.

He realizes the authority given him. Makes a per-formance of sharpening the knife. He carves with his tongue crawling round his top lip, like a child in the effort of concentration.

I suppose Anthony's drink is to blame. For a second, the room is both behind me and ahead of me. Either way I'm not in it. Not in this rive of time, this split instant, while Guy carefully slices away with the knife.

It's much noisier, people scurry round me, carrying platters. Dogs underfoot belch and yelp. Heavy scent competes with the smell of sweat. Across the table is a man with lace at his cuffs and throat, a man with very pale blue, serious eyes. He's the only one not shoving food into his face.

Then.

Then the people vanish. Everything's normal.

'No thank you, Anthony. I won't have any more wine for the moment.' My hand is a protective lid over the glass.

How many dinners did Milo Loughnian eat in this room? I doubt turkeys were around then. Perhaps a goose. Melissa was right to have wanted a goose. A goose would have pleased Milo. I'm certain. It's as if by jerking the house so violently into life, we've shaken up time, spilled over into a different year.

We haven't even picked up our knives or forks to begin when Adelaide knocks over the gravy boat. As well as the nasty brown stain besmirching Melissa's white linen cloth, Guy goes gorilla about his table. He makes the incident worse by much elaborate mopping up, then inverts a plate under the gravy stain. 'The mahogany. The patina,' he cries, panting like a dog after a bitch on heat. The cloth bears a malignant mole between the Brussels and the fantail potatoes.

'It wasn't my fault,' says Adelaide, her phoney accent more throaty than ever. She leans towards Guy and puts her hand on his knee. She's in the same problem area as Amy and myself. I don't think *she'd* have got the turkey out of the conservatory, let alone all the way to the Street-Langtons' dining-room. 'There's nothing to worry about, you sweet man. I feel quite sleepy. How about you?'

'Fresh as a cold shower,' says Guy, leaping up to shift her hand. He hotches his chair further away, rolls his head around, like a disorientated rubber-necked turtle emerging from the sea. Adelaide leans heavily back to try and make contact with him again. Unfortunately she's sitting on the faulty chair which Guy had identified earlier. The repair, on which too late she discovers she's leaning, hinges outwards with a gruesome crunch. Adelaide goes back with it.

Guy leans on the table and sobs in despair. 'My table and now my chair.'

'Don't worry, old chap,' says Anthony. 'I know a man. Give it the works. For next to nothing. Owes me a favour.' He helps lever Adelaide upright again.

'I long for,' says Grace, dreamily, 'the year two thousand and one. I shall be a woman of the last century. Become like a Victorian. I've never quite lived my life in the here and now. It's always been in the past or the future. I shall become focused at last.'

The strictures of poverty are not on this day confining Grace to the realm of the totally sober either.

Cob eats in silence, as if he's feeding a conveyor belt,

his pale eyes racing round the plate from turkey to stuffing to sausages. Cob probably never has a proper meal on his own. It'll be crisps and chocolate bars. I wish I could think of something comforting to say to him. To make him feel less lonely. Anything I'd come out with would sound stupid.

Amy holds out her arms and cries, 'Bless you all.' She waves her wineglass round her head. Luckily she's already drunk most of the first issue. 'A toast to our communal feast,' she says.

'You've been at the cooking sherry,' says Guy, and won't raise his glass. 'I hope none of this will take long. I've things to do.'

Melissa is spitting out bits of turkey. I wonder if the light in the hall was too dim to locate all the fluff off the carpet. I spot, nestling among the balls of sausage-meat stuffing, a lump of earth, likely to have dropped off a shoe. We collected it by mistake. We can only be grateful there's no badly-behaved dog living here, or what else might we have gathered up?

'Isn't this all lovely?' Amy squeaks, her chicks all gathered in, under the protective wings of the old house. 'At one.'

Anthony looks at us all coldly. He sees us littering his apartment. Without style.

'The Christmas we spent at St Moritz was the best.'

'Oh,' says Grace. 'Don't you like it here?'

'It's lovely,' says Anthony, smiling charmingly. He leans over and strokes Grace's hand, as if she were not an old woman at all. 'In the circumstances.' He looks pointedly at Adelaide.

Grace stares at her wrist where Anthony's fingers have been. She momentarily closes her eyes. Then, filled with new life, she passes behind the chairs, flinging extra Brussels onto plates. She looks exhausted but fulfilled. With less of Anthony's stylish hospitality in the kitchen, she'd be less of the first, and more of the second.

Amy, eager for intellectual interchange in true communal spirit, keeps throwing starter questions into the pool. A couple of openers go unchallenged. Amy floats another opportunity for intellectual interchange. 'If art *reflects* society, how can it also *influence* culture?'

'We've had the best of art,' says Guy. 'Been over for two hundred years in my opinion.'

'Yes?' Amy says, refusing to be daunted. 'Explain yourself.' At least *someone* is discussing.

'Stop prattling, woman.' Guy tastes his wine, pulls a face, and prods suspiciously at his pudding. Maybe he also had a bad experience with turkey extras.

'Give the presents out, Guy.' Adelaide gets bossy. She waves her pudding fork at him, coyly.

'Let me chew my way through this sludge,' he says. The pudding Grace made was not enough for so many of us. Anthony picked up a second with the turkey.

Eventually, Christmas gets even to Guy. He blossoms with the benevolence of playing Santa. Melissa produces a Father Christmas hat from a drawer, and Anthony shudders.

'What have we here? Ho ho.' Guy slowly draws out the first package, teasing us like children.

Amy rolls her eyes towards the ceiling, and Melissa giggles. 'My grandad was always drunk by now as well,' she observes.

I recognize the present I get as the one Cob brought, because I took note of the wrapping paper when he arrived. It's a sketch by Amy she'd consigned to a bin. He's mounted and framed it in pine and now it looks important, as if it were a doodle by Rembrandt himself. Amy is amazed. Strange that Cob could have been both so sensitive to see its potential, and so creative. Tonight is the start of the rest of my life. Tonight, I have

71

grown up at last. 'Yes, Anthony. Yes, I would like some more wine thank you.'

Because Anthony puts on a Christmas CD, versions of traditional carols so modern we can't recognize what they were originally, we don't hear the rain. Only Cob seems to be listening to it. Not until there's a bolt of thunder are we aware of the storm. Anthony switches off the CD and we listen in silence to the rain hitting the window with increasing spite. We gaze out into the gloom of the evening. Melissa draws the curtains, but the damage is done. The darkness has infected us. The sorrows of this house bear down, and I feel a communal misery and frustration that's not all of our making. There's a massive roll of thunder overhead.

'I want to go home,' says Guy. Anthony fills up his glass.

'We're right behind you,' says Adelaide. 'Coffee at your place.' She giggles. She's got to the stage where everything she says she finds amusing. Grace gazes sadly at the wreckage of her generously created gift to the house, her perfect Christmas dinner. Strange how the smell of turkey fat and Brussels sprouts lingers on, no longer delicious. I guess most of us are planning to leave the washing-up to Anthony.

Amy is not yet defeated. 'To the library,' she cries, and picking up her glass leads us across the hall. She's quite deliberate about how she advances her feet.

The third part of our day. The first was full of hope, it was tentative, it held out for possibilities of joy and transformation. Amy and I were happy. The second was the way of man, the hedonist and material pursuit of pleasure, the shovelling-in of food with gluttony and not appreciation, which reduces us all and scars the spirit. There is no child in this house to channel magic.

What is the third part?

It's that from which we shy away. Pain. I shall wonder later if it wasn't the most important part of the day. As we walk across the gloomy, cold hall to Guy's apartment, there's a sense of foreboding. Is it but an illusion the phoenix can rise from the ashes of the fire? Has there ever been a victory from a flood?

The very moment Guy opens the door, the ceiling comes plunging down.

The exquisite plaster lies in myriad pink and gold debris. Fragments of paint float down, giant Disney snowflakes to land on the gilt furniture and walnut tables, drawing them into the misery of the ceiling. It's a miracle that none of us is underneath.

Cob, first to recover, dashes into the hall and up the stairs, collecting receptacles on the way. The rest of us gaze in dismay.

Guy stares, with tears trickling obscenely down his cheeks. Heavily, he whispers, 'We must preserve the ceiling. Every last piece. We must save the ceiling.' You'd think he was talking about the Sistine chapel.

Whatever Cob does upstairs stems the water and we can get into the room. We gather the pieces of plaster, picking up each piece knowing it to be fragile, and pile it in one corner. We dust off what we cannot save. Anthony sobers up impressively and goes to help Cob deal with buckets on the top floor.

Amy smiles, a secret smile, out of character. I realize it pleases her to see us working together. For her, the tragedy is almost worth the communal drive. We push back the litter, mop up water and dust chairs. 'A bit of a flood won't daunt us,' Amy says, 'not when we're all pulling on the same rope.'

The mutilated plaster lies in heaps on the floor, pink, white and cerulean blue like icing chipping from God's wedding cake. The disfigured ceiling cries, as if

73

a beautiful woman has been slashed across the face, the brown scars above us, dark as old blood. There's a pain in my chest because something has happened that cannot be reversed. Like a fatal car crash. Guy leans like a zombie against the window-frame, unable to get his mind round how his life has collapsed. This is the beginning of a slow decay. We could be in sight of the end of anyone living in this house. The Philosopher's House is disintegrating faster than Guy can keep up with mending it.

The Forth bridge is kids' play compared to this.

Chapter Seven

Guy summons us to his library on Boxing morning. We sit on dusty chairs, and try not to scrunch the shards of ceiling we failed to retrieve yesterday.

'I have to make decisions,' he says ominously. Amy quivers, not only with anticipation, but with pleasure that we're together again so soon. She's made turkey sandwiches to sustain, intending to prolong the fellowship as long as possible. From above come thumps and thuds. Guy's found a man called Bert to carry out a temporary repair on the roof, in case it rains again. Bert's patching it from the inside, because he's not covered by insurance to go on the roof. His insurance limitations may result from being accident prone. When he came through the front door with his ladder, he failed to lower it sufficiently, so the end went through the glass fanlight above. As he lugged it out, hauling on the bottom rung, he misjudged the power of leverage, and the top end went into free fall skidding down the door, finally getting wedged in the letter-box. I hope Bert's having better luck in the roof space.

Guy's face is grey, the furrows defined more emphatically than ever. He doesn't mess about.

'Saving the library is the most important thing in my life. Paramount. That will cost. Cost a great deal.

Therefore,' he pauses and looks round at us. I feel like a piece of carrion waiting to be selected. 'The apartments must be sold.'

There's no sharp intake of breath. No cry. The news is expected.

'Only reasonable path. No alternative but to give you notice. You'll have first option to purchase. Of course.'

Is this where *reasoning* has led Guy? Is it *good* that three people could lose their homes to save a decorative ceiling?

I see the hurt in Amy's face, and know it's more than her home under threat. It's the commune. The spiritual identity of the house.

'You know perfectly well, Guy,' she says, 'that I, at least, have no capital.'

'I have to say,' adds Adelaide, 'that my money is extensively tied up. My late husband was an extraordinarily prudent man.'

'If only you'd been off the bottle at the time,' muses Grace with compassion, and no malice, 'then he might have been less devious.'

'I was out of sorts with my back.' Adelaide is naturally defensive.

'On your back more like,' murmurs Anthony.

'This place has been our home for thirty years.' There's no accusation in Grace's voice. 'I don't have a bean. I can only just afford a little dry sherry. We're never intoxicated these days. The one good thing about all this, really. Poverty has saved us from our little excesses.' It's Good Friday for Grace again, without Easter to follow.

But I'm wrong. Grace clasps her hands and whispers to me, 'I'm certain the Lord will lift his hand. Just this once.'

Cob, against the window, the light behind him casting his face in shadow, stares coldly at Guy. He no longer looks an elf. More of a satyr, with imaginary horns in his hair. I can't tell what he's thinking.

'It's not *my* fault the bloody ceiling's come down.' Guy has so little imagination on behalf of others he can't begin to see what pain he's inflicting.

There's a noise outside the door and Bert crashes into the room, tripping over the edge of the carpet. 'Excuse me,' he says, 'but do you have a screwdriver at all? I've been unfortunate enough to bend mine crooked as I prised open my sandwich tin.'

'I'm not paying you to eat. It's not even ten o'clock,' says Guy.

'If I don't eat on the hour regular I go dizzy up the ladder,' explains Bert.

'There's a tool-box in the shed at the back,' says Guy, not offering to show him.

Anthony, at the far end of the room, away from the rest of us, leans elegantly against the panelled shutters of the window. He waits until Guy looks in his direction, then one eyebrow arches upward. It's a command. Guy walks over to Anthony. I'm the only one who spots the waggling eyebrow, and sidle over to the nearby bookshelf, taking a close interest in the lower shelves. It's the travel section, which is not exactly *How to Visit Nepal on a Shoestring*, but things like *Travels With a Donkey*, and *As I Walked Out One Midsummer Morning*. All the valuable antique books are at the far end, near to Guy's writing-table. My eyes scan the titles but my ears are open to what Anthony says.

'Put a proposition to you, old chap.' Anthony momentarily abandons his style, and takes on pseudo Guy-speak. 'You've certainly got a taker for my apartment. Not a man to try and beat you down either, you know. Better still, how would you feel about me buying one of the other apartments, and running it into our

77

own? Would suit *you* better. More like one house than a block of flats. Cut the inconvenience of showing people round. No problem of a mortgage where I'm concerned, either.'

Guy stares at him, gobsmacked. He's not accustomed to people having ready money. Respectable people simply don't have it. They're burdened by their inheritance. The suggestion's not sinking in too fast.

'Well, I don't know. Have to think about it. Have to give the tenants a bit of time, you know.'

'Of course. Of course.' Anthony extends his hand as if to shake on a deal, but Guy, looking dazed, puts his hand behind his back. Something, far back in Guy's ancestry, seems to be reminding him to behave like a gentleman. Privilege carries responsibilities. I doubt if there's much reasoning going on in Guy's head. Wavering, he turns round and says, 'The first and most essential intention is to preserve the library.'

'Absolutely.' Anthony winks, and nods sideways to show his sympathy and understanding. If he nods like that too much he'll end up seeing an osteopath. 'You might like me to put in a swimming-pool. Covered, of course.'

'A *swimming*-pool?' It's as if he'd said *cess*pool.

'Always an investment. Classy. Sauna room as well, of course. What do you say? Wouldn't cost you a penny. Put up the value of the flats no end.'

Guy shudders. 'It would encourage frogs.'

Anthony catches my eye and grins, a special person-to-person grin. We can share the joke that Guy is an ignorant old bat.

There's terror on Guy's face, the fear of losing all he has. I regret I conspired with Anthony by smiling back at him.

Adelaide's got her second wind. 'I shall lay it on the line to you. We have our rights, and will find out what

78

they are. Very timely for you that most of the leases are coming up for renewal.' She limps to a conclusion. 'What we need, Guy, is to find another way.'

'I need a huge amount of money, Adelaide. These restoration people don't come cheap. Even the little pillock up there in the roof is skinning me. This is my heritage. I'm responsible. If I don't preserve the library with its glorious ceiling, then . . .' He tails off, but we know he means he'll be nothing if all that goes. Because that's all he is. The house, and its long-gone philosopher.

'There's an offer for one apartment on the table,' Guy says, weakening already, 'and possibly a second.'

The three women look round in amazement, not having been lurking in earshot. Amy and Adelaide size each other up, then frown and look accusingly at Guy.

'Anthony's made an offer.'

'Who else has?'

'Myself, again. For either one of the others. If you don't wish to purchase yourselves, of course.' Anthony sits back in his chair, smiling modestly. Pride in his bank balance has overcome any embarrassment at robbing single women of their protecting roof. This morning he's less beautiful, less glossy. There are scornful lines joining his nose and mouth I've not noticed before. His hands, with perfectly filed and buffed nails, rest lightly on the arms of the chair, quite relaxed now, but, like spring traps, with the potential to grab and claw.

Melissa giggles. 'You see, Anthony really loves this house. He's going to have it all, one day.'

Anthony looks up to the ceiling and tilts his chair back. I wish he'd overbalance. He has done, in a way.

Guy says, 'So that's the game, is it? You want the bloody lot.' Cob, like me, looks relieved. Guy understands now, and won't relinquish his inheritance to Anthony Street-Langton. 'Your deal's off.'

'Look here. A figure of speech, wasn't it darling?' Anthony glowers at Melissa. 'Of course we'd love the house but that's not at all what we're up to. Nothing further from my mind.' His eyes are smiling now, crinkly, amusing, teasing us to respond. Only Grace smiles back, taken in.

'We'll have to find another way.' Guy stares out of the window, seeking inspiration from his vanishing land, the surrounding fields that were once his estate.

'Hooray for Guy,' says Amy and hugs him. Tersely, he brushes her off. It takes him time to get his face back in control, he's overcome by his own innate sense of what is right.

'Vegetables,' Amy says. 'We could grow our own vegetables.' Her face is alight now. 'We'll be a co-operative.' I don't know if this is one up on a commune, but it's certainly got Amy alight.

Grace claps her hands. 'Broad beans. Little tender broad beans. And sweetcorn.'

'Cattle fodder,' says Guy, 'sweetcorn is.'

'What about avocados?' Adelaide's swept away too. Silly old cow.

'There's one thing you could do.' Cob looks pale. 'You could do up my cottage. I'll be at university after the summer. In the meantime I could doss down on the top floor.'

I can't bear to think of Cob leaving the only home he has.

'There's obligations,' says Guy. 'An agreement. Otherwise I'd have sold that off already.'

'I thought you took me in out of kindness,' whispers Cob. He's white, drained of the one kind act he thought he'd received since being on his own. It has seeped away as from a wound. 'Kindness?' Cob repeats, giving Guy another chance.

'Hardly,' says Guy, and looks as if he wants to tell Cob to belt up. 'Why else would you think I'd take a little runt like you into my house?'

Cob walks out of the room.

'But it's given me an idea,' says Guy, hardly noticing what he's done to Cob. 'The stable block.'

'My studio?' Now Amy's shocked.

'No written agreement. No-one else has access to extra accommodation.'

'No.' Amy swallows. 'No, of course not.'

Guy says, 'At least that's a start.'

'It'll save all our bacons for a bit, dear,' says Adelaide.

Grace says nothing and the tears fall down her face. I can see her hands pressed together under the table. Even now, she's praying for Amy. I could cry as well. 'It'll never be *enough*,' she whispers. 'The day will come when we shall all lose our homes.'

Amy's gone missing when I get up next morning. There's been snow in the night. It's worked its magic, as ever. The gardens spread out before me, virgin and pure, and very still. Beyond the wall the fields are flat and smooth and will only come alive if the sun comes out. The hedges look black and stark and eternally inert.

The front door's not locked. The outside door no longer has its chain across. Amy's gone to her studio to paint the courtyard under snow. Her last picture. I imagine her picking her way around the edge so she doesn't break its beauty with scrunchy footprints. I take breakfast to her, a couple of large bacon butties and some coffee.

Amy isn't painting. She's sitting on a chair at the window, staring out on the snow. Not the window that looks over the courtyard, but the one at the other end, the huge one she had put in. It's full of pale morning sky, and there's no shadow cast on her face. She's very erect and her hands lie passively in her lap. Her wild hair's subdued, some of its electricity seeped away. I know Amy is bereft, even though her mouth and eyes are their usual unmoving selves. She's mourning her studio. She loves it, and she's going to give it up. I hand her the butty, but she only eats half, so I finish it off, because I'm mourning for her now, as well as the studio, and I need the comfort. Her painting makes up for so much. It's her child, her lover, it's her soul. Poor darling Amy. She doesn't say anything.

'You could paint in the conservatory.'

'It faces south. The light will never be right.'

'No. Of course not.'

Amy goes to look out of the other window on to the courtyard. 'It's too grand for me anyway. I'm not good enough to have a wonderful studio. I haven't sold anything for months.'

'Van Gogh *never* sold anything.'

'Everything he painted sells for more noughts than I've got paintbrushes now. He was an artist. I'm just a practical woman.'

'Yes.' I say *yes* because it's what she wants to hear. It's not the truth. The last thing Amy is, is practical. I don't know if she's an artist. All I know is that I wish more than anything I could comfort her. She never deserves to be hurt.

'I shouldn't care. Art should be for its own sake. Not for me to succeed. The ego isn't a creative element.' She stands up and hauls out two of her canvases. 'Help me get them over to the house, Charis, and we'll make a start here.' She elongates her neck, though it'll never be swanlike. Her face comes close to lighting up. Her fountain of generosity within is bubbling up again. 'I'm going to make this place into the most wonderful studio apartment you've ever seen. It will inform a life.'

'I'll help you clean if you want,' Cob says, when he sees Amy and me struggling across the yard. 'Guy likes to see me earning my keep.' He looks at me, and I wish I'd done something with my hair. I couldn't care less. He looks as if he hasn't washed. Is anything ever going to go right in my life?

By lunch-time the snow has melted. Ethereal as all joys. I'm worried about Grace. The threat of homelessness seems too heavy a burden for her frail frame, and there may not be a god to rescue her. I get to their door on the first floor when out she comes, remarkably chirpy. 'Taking Bert his peppermint tea,' she whispers. 'He needs its soothing qualities. You can see he appreciates it because he drinks it slowly. To make it last. On his last bit of patching to the roof, before the tiling experts arrive. Guy never thinks to give him a hot drink. Bert only has that unwholesome flask. Coated inside with a brown film that flakes off into his drink.' Grace, like a priestess carrying a libation, holds aloft with both hands a china beaker with primroses around the brim. We move up to the top floor.

'Adelaide is low with the influenza. Can take only consommé with sherry. At least consommé is cheap.'

'Down in a sec,' says Bert, not looking as pleased as he should to see Grace.

'*So* interesting. Talking to people from different walks of life,' whispers Grace, cocking her head towards Bert. Her whisper is louder than she means, and Bert glowers down at us malevolently.

Grace waits to hand him the drink personally, and I wander to the window to look out on the grounds of Loughnian House from this great height. Only the village is in view, the rest is fields. Fields which were once the Loughnian estate. Still some garden remains, quite a large area to the front, a spinney to the left, the Italian garden to the right, at Guy's end of the house, and more grass beyond that where Amy is considering growing the vegetables. Something unusual in that grass catches my eye. A pattern of modified greens. Perhaps due to uneven melting of the snow. Truly a design, not a random mottling. Squares, smaller shapes and a circle, of a richer stain, of lusher growth. I stare at it for ages, and wonder why there's a pattern like that.

'Grace?' Together we stare down. 'You do see it?'

Grace absent-mindedly drinks the tea she's brought for Bert. 'Yes, I see it, dear. It looks . . . yes, it must be. The abbey herb garden. Certain. Yes. This is where herbs were cultivated long ago. Their enrichment is still with us. What a miracle we didn't dig it up for potatoes.'

Grace grasps me by the arm and we go down to see more closely, leaving a scowling Bert stuffing a hefty cheese sandwich into his mouth. I hope he's not come over dizzy without his peppermint tea.

We kneel down and stroke the blades of grass, especially vigorous grass, fed for centuries by the plenitude of composted goodness. 'I can feel it, you know. The holiness. This is a healing place. The monks grew herbs here. Guy may have told you the house was built on the site of a derelict abbey. Do I mean nuns? Thyme for cooking perhaps, but hyssop and chervil for healing, for their soothing. Charis, herbs have enhanced lives. Brought happiness. That's what we'll do again. I must learn exactly what there would have been. We don't want anything foreign. The Lord is wondrous thoughtful, I find.

'I shall be so happy creating this garden, discovering

a mystical place six centuries past. Where women were pure and visionary. The spiritual light within them bright and clear. I shall not be confused in this place. I shall be happy, and so will others who can share it with me. We must celebrate.'

Grace and Adelaide's apartment has a cupboard-like space, which is the kitchen, contrived from a fraction of another room. It overlooks the courtyard.

On the cooker stands a pan of clear soup. On the table beside it, an inch of sherry in a bottle. 'She's feeling better anyway,' says Grace, dividing the sherry unevenly between three glasses which she puts on a tray.

Adelaide is writing at a large desk, wearing a cerise dress which swathes across her chest and abdomen like brocade on a Turkish ottoman, and a green-lined tennis visor protecting her eyes from glare. The desk seems very much hers, ostentatious with ormolu-crusted corners, and a silk-padded chair. On the other side of the room is a small davenport, walnut with golden knots and curls within the wood. I'm certain this belongs to Grace. On top is a diary, with a heart-shaped lock on it.

'I can't wait for ever for the old buffer to come to his senses,' Adelaide says over her shoulder. 'One has to *make* things happen. Be responsible for one's happiness. With the constant threat of financial deprivation one must look ahead. Oh, it's you, Charis.' She takes a sherry, one slightly fuller than the other two.

'An advertisement,' she explains. 'Can't make up my mind between the 'Saturday Rendezvous' on page nine of the Weekend section of *The Times*, and 'Encounters' in the Style section of *The Sunday Times*.' She has copies before her of each from the previous week.

'Wittier than the ads in the local paper. Also, they

come from a safe distance. No risk of an embarrassing appointment with a neighbour. Those looking for Encounters seem to be racier than those wanting a Rendezvous. The men who advertise in 'Encounters' use the word curvaceous a lot. It all comes down to class. What do you think GSOH means?'

'If they can't spell *gosh*,' says Grace, 'they must be quite old.'

'N/S? WLTM?'

'You don't want any foreigners,' says Grace. 'They won't eat the same dinners.'

'Attractive lady of September years. Yes, that's rather good, or does it sound too old? Lady in her experienced prime? No, that might attract the sexually incontinent. I wouldn't want more than once a week now. Ten days even better. Attractive lady of ageless looks. Yes. A hint of being on the wrong side of fifty, but it doesn't matter.'

'You *are* doing well,' says Grace, finishing her sherry, and swapping her empty glass with Adelaide's. '*GSOH* means good sense of humour,' she adds, her mind clearing beautifully.

'Good sense of humour is what they all want,' Adelaide observes, 'which is odd considering how few people in the daily round have little more than the capacity to laugh at obvious jokes. How few know even the meaning of irony?'

Adelaide believes she *is* of the few. 'I've put ESOH. E for excellent. Shows the original mind. Seeks cultured gentleman, of similar means. We won't be more specific than that. For companionable afternoons out. Make that days out. Afternoons have connotations. *Must be solvent.*'

Adelaide gets up from the desk and moves over to the mirror between the windows. It reflects the glass on either side, making the room look even larger.

Admiringly, she strokes her hand down the length of her podgy front, over the generous undulations of cerise brocade.

'One of life's great mysteries,' she muses, 'is why men love boobs, go wild with lust over them, but totally ignore the superboob, which is the ageing woman's stomach. It's all there, the soft floppiness, the pendular tendency, the ability to sway from side to side, even with an inverted nipple, and above all, twice the size.'

'Men don't have your imagination, dear,' Grace explains.

'I think,' Adelaide decides, 'I shall need to read this over, several times. Carefully, and when entirely sober.' She puts the advert in one of the small drawers in the top of her desk, and locks it.

Grace, alerted to tidying mode, swoops on her diary still lying on top of the davenport, and opens the top drawer. This, too, has a key. These sisters have secrets from each other still.

I love looking in windows lit at dusk, seeing into people's rooms, speculating on their lives, extending my experiences, if only vicariously. I used to believe this was a sinister activity, but the dictionary describes vicarious as *acting for another* or *experienced imaginatively through another person*. Now I have no qualms about it. So I'm not slow to take a good look into Grace's drawer, while it's open.

Momentarily, she picks up a photo, bent round the edges and dissolving into sepia age and sadness. I glimpse it is of three people, but I can't make out who they might be. Lightly, she touches it with her finger, almost a caress. Beneath it lies a package, a brown manila envelope heavily secured with Sellotape. The name on the envelope is face down. Stored envelopes almost always have the name and address uppermost.

It's automatic. It's how people put envelopes down. What's in this envelope, that would disturb Grace too much to read its name? Will the day come when she will have to? I speculate there is more to Grace than the sapless spinster she might appear.

Chapter Eight

It should be the work of half a day to clear the studio, then after a lick of paint it will become an apartment. I'm wrong. It takes until the end of my stay. At the same time, contrary to all expectations, Mother's pantomime doesn't fold. She's still got something going with Nick, the junior electrician, so she doesn't want me around anyway. It must be her last throw. I'm pleased, not only for her, but because I like it here with Amy. Being with her makes me feel relevant. She's warm and doesn't have expectations of me.

I only wish I felt as comfortable with Cob. I'm inadequate when he's anywhere near. Unfortunately he appears to have forgotten I've got green eyes.

All day we move Amy's paints, jars, prepared boards, unsold paintings and useful props like the wicker chair and unusual glass bottles over to the house. Guy, in grudging appreciation of Amy's sacrifice, makes available a cupboard for storage. More of a room than a cupboard, with a window on to the hall of his apartment, because that had once been the servants' back hall, and the cupboard was the butler's pantry. It smells of mouse. More than one. With undue fuss, he boards up the window from his side, so Amy won't be able to spy on him. This she would never consider doing, but it might have been a valuable source of experience now denied to me.

Melissa trails through the hall as we cart the stuff in, and elegantly sways over to look at a painting. 'Those colours,' she says, and seems to drink them in. It's of roses, created in Amy's night-painting period, and the moonlight makes the flowers vibrant against black leaves. The painting's not about roses at all, it's about hope and vision, how darkness and unhappiness can shape beauty.

'They remind me of my Gran's garden. Roses grew all over the back porch. Yellow ones. In the summer we'd have our tea on the table under them. All among the flowerpots and the bicycles and nets of onions. Anthony would have hated it. Could I buy that, do you think?'

Amy wobbles her head, and makes a quick flick with her right forearm to show indecision. 'You don't have to be kind.'

'I know what it's like to move,' says Melissa. 'What it's like to leave home.'

'Please, *have* it,' says Amy, grateful someone likes her work.

I help Melissa carry the painting through her front door.

'I know Anthony won't like it at all.' There's something stubborn about Melissa. When we get it to the kitchen she leans back on the kitchen table and closes her eyes, tilting her face to the ceiling. 'Mum was only doing her best,' she says. 'She honestly thought I deserved it.'

I don't know what to say. She might cry. I'm out of my depth. Luckily Melissa pulls herself together. 'Right Charis. You go and help Amy, and I'll bring you both a nice cup of tea.' Why is a cup of tea always nice? Have I ever been offered a nasty cup of tea? Anthony would disapprove of Melissa using clichés.

Crisis averted, I could kick myself for not encouraging her, not finding out much more. To add to the storehouse of my life.

The removal of clutter from the tack-room reveals a door directly through to the stables. Guy comes to inspect. Cob leans against the window awaiting instructions. He's picking dirt out from under his fingernails. Perhaps one should rejoice?

'The studio will be the drawing-room, and the stalls can be bedroom and kitchen.' Guy looks at Amy to confirm the plan. 'The other stall will provide excellent storage space. Ample storage is a selling feature.'

'You can't have a drawing-room without a dining-room,' says Amy, 'because that's where you withdraw from.'

'You're surely not going to call it a lounge,' sneers Guy. You sometimes think his top lip will disappear up his nostrils when he talks like that.

'It'll always be the studio to me,' says Amy, perfectly calm.

Guy hobbles off. 'I'm going to see the insurance man,' he says. 'I do have insurance on the place, but they'll try to wriggle out of paying up. Always do. Parasites. Out of the same cesspool as bank managers and plumbers.'

Amy yells after Guy, 'You've forgotten the bathroom. Again.'

'Tell Cob to plumb one in,' bellows Guy over his shoulder, and disappears.

Amy looks round, fighting her many hurts. She closes her elephant-grey eyes, swaying slightly. 'I'm trying to visualize what's for the best,' she says. 'I want a lot of yellow. I want it to be a happy room.' She swallows tears she's sucked back from behind her eyes.

'Guy says I'm to clean through first, so you've got

time to plan.' Cob levers himself off the window-frame, strips off a sweater and says to me, 'You can stay and help if you want.'

I try to think of an excuse to get away. Then wonder how green my eyes are looking today. So I take the cloth he offers, and start to wash the paintwork.

'What music you like then? What's your best group?'

'Haven't got one, really.' I've never been to a pop concert, so I can't impress him with live gigs. What the girls at school watch on the telly is more about sex than sound. Better be honest. 'I've been to two symphony concerts with the school.' Amazingly, that goes down well.

'Dad used to play the violin. He played it a treat. I liked that. Played the clarinet as well.'

'Did he play Mozart? I went to a clarinet quintet last term. It was lovely.' I notice Cob's dad seems to be in the past.

'Expect he did. I didn't really bother with names. Just liked to listen. Got some of the tapes he bought. He liked all sorts.'

I wait to hear more about Cob's dad. But no more comes and I'm too shy to ask. It's difficult when people have died. 'So what group's *your* best?'

'Haven't got one either.' He half smiles. We've both been pretending. That makes him easier to talk to.

'Doing A levels in the summer?'

'Yes.'

'Me too.'

He says, 'I've applied to Sussex. For philosophy. Don't think they'll ask for impossible grades.'

'Because of Milo?'

'I wanted to do that before I even knew about him.'

'Where do you go to school then?'

'In the pits. Not really worth four buses a day. We failed our Ofsted. You should see the others that go there. Nobody talks to me because I want to go to university. Think I'm off the planet.' He stops working and stares out of the window. 'Teachers aren't any better. Don't get much help from them. Don't think I'll get the grades. Doubt *they've* got the grades.'

Since he doesn't bother to ask, I tell him, 'I've applied to Durham. But I'll be lucky. History. Though I might switch to English. They'll want impossible grades. I'll never get that. I expect I'll end up working in a supermarket. On the checkout.'

'Depends how badly you want it, doesn't it?'

'I do want it. Really badly.'

'Well you're at a plushy private school. Amy told me.'

'Not plushy at all. I bet our lot are thicker than yours.'

He says nothing. He doesn't care about me enough to try to talk me into a positive frame of mind. Cob scarcely looks up. He's got power over me. The power to make me feel silly and scared of him. I wish he hadn't.

Bert comes lumbering across the courtyard. 'Seen Mr Loughnian at all?'

'Not a bit of him,' says Cob.

'Had a mishap in the library. Could you take a look-see?'

Apparently Bert, having finished his patching of the roof, felt curious and decided to inspect what remains of the library ceiling, the residue of plaster beneath the surface decoration. Guy's taken the books down to dry out, and Bert leaned his ladder against the top shelf. He put his sandwich tin *on* the shelf, in case he came over dizzy on the top rung.

We stare up at where the ladder points the way to Bert's little accident.

'Unfortunately, my elbow slipped. Being greasy. Got

93

caught up in the butter at breakfast. Unexpected like, the sandwich tin went straight through the wall. Like a coffin on its way at the crematorium. Never come across that before.'

'How can it have done?' Cob asks. 'There'd be solid brick.'

'Don't ask *me*.' Bert begins to sound self-righteous. 'It might have thrown me off the ladder.'

Cob goes up the ladder himself. 'More than a hole. There's a deliberate cavity here. Perhaps a primitive safe. A place to hide valuables.'

'Any gold and jewels up there now?' Bert is sarcastic.

'No. No. Tell you what, Bert. Why don't you get a bit of board from the shed? There's some paint there too. You could repair this before Guy gets back. He'll be none the wiser.'

Bert leaves, catching his sleeve on the door handle as he goes. He catapults back into the room.

'Right,' says Cob, when Bert's finally gone. 'There *is* something here, Charis. A box. Sort of casket. I'm bringing it down.'

The box is polished rosewood, with sharp brass corners. The brass is tarnished now, but the wood looks sound. It breathes dust, drowsy with time.

'Why would that box be hidden up there?'

'We'll find out. It won't be Guy's. He has a safe behind some books. Wouldn't need to hide something up there,' says Cob. 'Go and see Guy's not lurking anywhere.'

From the courtyard I check not even Grace is at her kitchen window. We dash across the yard to Cob's cottage.

This was perhaps a groom's quarters, not built for comfort, only shelter. There's one downstairs room, presumably with a bedroom above. A small high window, for ventilation, not a view, and a boarded-up iron fireplace. To replace it, a chipped space-heater with frayed flex. A single gas ring in the corner. Plaster walls with an optimistic pale blue wash. I expected Cob to exist in a tip, but everything is amazingly neat. There are two armchairs, a card-table with a dark blue cloth. Piled neatly on the table are three chocolate bars and six packets of crisps. As I imagined. The grey tinge of his skin goes with an absence of calabrese and savoy. As with Amy's apartment, there's a deficiency of plumbing. One tap in the corner over a tiny earthenware sink.

Cob dusts the box with his elbow, and tries to open it. There's no key.

'Was there a key with it?'

'Course not. I looked. Doubt we'll ever find that key now. Have to prise it open.'

'You might damage it.'

Cob looks at me witheringly. 'It's a perfectly ordinary box. But what's inside might be valuable.' He goes to work with a fork. Quite quickly he gets it open.

Disappointing, really. Inside are only letters. Yellow paper. Scrawled writing. Different scrawls. Boring, I think, but Cob is animated. Carefully he unfolds the first, and we look at the signature. The writing is spidery and ornate. Difficult to read.

'*Look* at that.'

Even I can pick out the name.

Milo Loughnian.

The hand of Milo Loughnian is here before us. As if he has this moment put down the pen and walked away. No-one has touched this paper since he did. It's hard to believe that last human touch was over two hundred years ago. I reach out to the page, tentative and unsure. It feels warm beneath my fingers, as if the words are alive.

'Why did he hide these away? You'd think they'd be in his desk, or wherever it was he left the diaries.'

'The diaries were public property really. In those days men wrote journals with a view to publishing them. Worldly matters. Politics. History. Philosophy. They weren't confessionals. On the other hand, these letters . . . There must be a reason for hiding them. Almost permanently, I'd have said.'

'Guy'll be pleased to have these.'

'Not until *I've* read them. Milo was my ancestor as well, you know. Mum always swore she was Loughnian blood. Same as Guy. So she claimed anyway. Don't know how she knew. Mother was a secretive woman. In many ways. There's questions I regret not asking now.'

He leans over the other letters, cautiously lifting the pages. There's something about the bones of his face, that area below the brow, that plane from cheek to chin. His bones are noble, almost as well-bred as Guy's superb head. They could be Loughnian bones. His mother may have been right. I can't read what the letter says though.

Cob is more confident. 'I'll decipher them in time. Guy will just have to wait.'

This afternoon, though Cob would prefer to go through Milo's cache of letters, Guy insists he gets down to some plumbing for the studio apartment bathroom. He's lost faith in Bert, even though he doesn't know about the accident in the library. After Guy admonished his insurance brokers this morning, he apparently stopped by at W. H. Smith and bought a do-it-yourself manual. It provided the answer to further unnecessary plumbing bills. After a quick flick through the relevant pages, he went to a hardware store and invested a modest sum in piping, wrenches,

96

flanges, washers, wadding and the cheapest shower head on the shelf.

'Nothing to it, Cob,' he says. 'Page ninety-seven onwards. The work of minutes.'

Not the work of minutes, but a day and a half. Half an hour after he's finished, water pours forth from the elbow connection with such force it's impossible to turn off the flood at source. Luckily, Cob, with huge strength and courage, manages to hold the pipe so the deluge goes through the window, and doesn't fill up the studio. It ranks with one of the labours of Hercules, but Guy fails to give credit for this. The outcome is that Guy has to call the fire brigade.

After this cheery band leaves, grateful that for once the situation isn't life-threatening, we're still having a bit of trouble with the pipes. The whole system starts to play up.

Adelaide storms into the studio. 'There's boiling water in my loo. It attacked my buttocks.'

'Ugh,' says Guy. Not certain whether his sympathy lies with Adelaide or the flush.

'Can't get a bloody shower now,' shouts Anthony from his window across the courtyard.

Melissa appears behind him. 'I don't like to complain of course, but there's more than pink tissue in the washing-machine.' Her delicate nose is still a quiver.

'I told you, Guy,' says Anthony a bit later, coming outside, 'give me a free hand and I'll build you not only a pool and sauna, but a laundry room as well. Get a new inlet from the mains. I know people at the water board. Take all the pressure off your system.'

I nudge Amy. 'The sauna will have a shower. Would suit you.'

'A pool,' says Grace, who has come out to back

up Adelaide. 'A *pool*. Symbolic purification. An opportunity for spiritual renewal.'

'A swimming-pool, sweetie,' Anthony points out, 'not your personal slice of the Ganges.'

Grace is undaunted. 'I shall have a new swimming cozzy. Turquoise, I think.'

'A damned swimming-pool is the last bloody thing we want,' says Guy. 'Duckweed and chlorine. You'll be wanting a new-fangled Jacuzzi next, something to knock your balls off.'

'Additionally,' says Anthony, 'your wiring is undeniably dodgy.'

Cob knocks on the conservatory window, and waves a plastic carrier bag in the air. 'Going to give Guy a couple of the letters. The only ones I've managed to read properly. You coming?'

'OK. But why two now? Why not wait until you've finished reading them all?'

'Because I can't wait to see his face when he sees these.'

'Yes?' Guy's shirt isn't properly tucked in, and there's a brown stain on his cuff. Looks like soup. I imagine Guy has a great deal of soup. Tinned. Packet for a change. Cob, with right on his side, strides into the library.

'I'm busy,' says Guy. 'Drafting an advertisement. How does this sound?' Ignoring Cob waving the bag at him, he reads aloud to us.

'Do you crave an harmonious lifestyle? Studio apartment for sale in pleasant rural area. In proximity to charming eighteenth-century house, a delightful hamlet and ten minutes by car from Safeway. Fifteen minutes to the station with lines to all reasonable towns, even London. An attractive and good sized drawing-room, exquisitely and expensively fitted kitchen, bedroom with views over the Hertfordshire countryside. And, of course, pristine bathroom. Would suit country-loving lady of reasonable years.'

His flowery tone goes ill with the air quality of the library, which is cold and smells permanently of dust and fungicide treatments to the roof.

He moves some papers to find the phone, to reveal a pile of bills. Jutting out at the bottom I spot estimates for rewiring the house, and more for a plumbing engineer. I'm dizzy with the excess of noughts.

'The studio won't be ready for weeks,' warns Cob. 'The plumbing could burst out at any time.'

'Priorities,' says Guy, pointing upwards. 'We're snug and watertight. Temporary ceiling. We no longer rely on the frail bodging of Bert. That man is joined by the umbilical cord to an accident. Men with scaffolding have been up on the tiles. The complete ceiling restoration awaits only the sale of the stable apartment.'

'You shouldn't scoff at Bert. He's unearthed some of Milo's letters.'

Guy's face is like an old movie, you could see each change come over him in jerky stages. Annoyance at being disturbed, reassessing what he's heard, disbelief, astonishment, elation, disbelief again.

'Say again.'

'Milo's letters. Hidden behind the plaster at the top of one of your bookcases.' Cob fishes out two letters from the plastic bag and puts them on Guy's desk. The old man stares at them, eventually stretching out one finger to touch the paper, just as I had done. Gingerly, as if stroking a moth, he opens them one after the other and checks the dates. He sits down and looks up at us.

Tears are rivuleting down his sagging cheeks. It's rather embarrassing. 'I never thought to see the day,' Guy mutters, 'when I would find anything else.'

'Read this one, then,' says Cob. 'Or do I have to decipher it for you?'

'You forget, Cob, that unlike you, I am familiar with his hand.' To prove that, he reads out loud.

> The twenty fifth day of September 1758
>
> My beloved Elizabeth,
>
> As I sit in my chair you are always here beside me. It is as if your spirit has left your body and has flown to meld with mine. Sometimes we lean towards each other and it is as if we physically touch. I cannot believe you are not thinking of me constantly. As I am of you. I hear your voice, low, and you whisper to me. As with music, what you tell me is in your own language. I hear it not within my ear but within my heart. Closer still.

'Drivelling idiot,' says Guy.

> I had never thought that our love could become real. I had resolved to put you out of my mind, though I was always a great way from accomplishing that. Even when I received your invitation to your house gathering. There were so many elegant faces there, I had not for a moment considered it would be me whom you would take to your bed. We lay entwined until the dawn. I did not sleep. I cannot put these things into words for they might become coarse, and of the language of ordinary men, other and less significant lovers.
>
> I wish no ill of any one, and certainly not now with the knowledge of such a pure and untainted love, but I cannot but encompass the hope that the day will come, at least some time in my life, when

you will be free and we can come together for all the world to know.

> Yours,
>> unresting, and forsaking all peace
>>> Milo Loughnian.

'I'm disappointed in you, Milo,' says Guy. 'How can a man with your fine mind write such rubbish?'

'This is the other one.' It is written in an elegant hand, with many flourishes, and wide spaces between words. Almost spidery, but the size of the lettering suggests a generous nature. I would say that this is a woman's hand. Guy finds this more difficult to work out, and Cob eventually reads it to him.

> The fourth day of October, 1758

My dear Milo,

This may be the saddest day of my life. First, because I have to write this letter, and second because of what has happened that causes me to communicate with you in these terms. For this reason I also return your most treasured letter.

Last week I received advance warning that my husband was to return from the war against Austria, as a result of grievous injury. But I had not expected to find his poor body so damaged. It is a crime that such a decent man should be brought so low because of his courage as a soldier. I am told he was believed to be so great a soldier it is his absence from the fighting that has rendered the Prussian army to its present desperate situation. We should now doubt the wisdom of their King to pursue the war with such diligence in the first instance.

He has told me that only his love for me caused him to cling to life in the fiercest moments of his pain and bleeding. Only my love for him can now heal him. I sat beside him this afternoon as he slept upon the day bed in my sitting room, and I have resolved that I must give my life over to his recovery, such as that may be. I fear he may yet lose his left leg.

Please understand me, dear Milo, when I tell you there cannot be another visit to me here, nor should I ever see you again. Such days of carefree games are over for me. I am become a serious woman.

Your affectionate friend
Elizabeth Fraser.

'Bloody hell,' says Guy and lifts his face to the ceiling, an expression of pain scooting across his face, like wine spilled on a good carpet, leaching and sinking into the surface, and spoiling it for ever. His life's work, Milo, the pearl of perfect intellect, is flawed. 'Mixed up with a woman,' he says, 'and one bloody well married at that. To a war hero.'

He looks through the window where the winter sun filters through the trees like translucent silver. Amy swings by, a sketch-pad under one arm, her box of paints in the opposite hand. She looks up as she passes and wobbles her head about in greeting as she can't wave. Her black hair bounces about her head like a lost swarm of bees. She's making for the Italian garden, to paint without her studio.

Guy shudders. He hates outside. It's the opposite of civilization. Nature's in control out there, not man. Especially in his garden, where so much has grown rampant. Enlightenment man understood that so well. Such men planned nature on their land, created their own civilized scapes. Capability Brown. Our only civilized piece of ground now is the Italian garden.

102

Even that's too outside for Guy. Which ought to, but doesn't, mean he's even more enlightened than those who lived in the eighteenth century.

I can see how he's thinking. Guy experiences his first and probably only sensation of maternalism, which is a more intimate emotion than paternity. Milo, together with the journals, is his child, his baby, and he knows he can do nothing but love it, however it behaves. He cannot turn his back on forgiveness. He prays silently to an absent god within his head that there's nothing worse to come. Then, like a mother, he experiences an additional aspect to his life, another facet, one more exciting than his own. One more painful.

The night before I leave Loughnian House I don't sleep well, and wake up feeling sad. I go to the window to see if the weather fits my mood, as it always did for Jane Eyre. I don't expect anyone else to be awake. I'm wrong.

Anthony Street-Langton is walking round the house in a black tracksuit. Is there anything in which that man doesn't look dishy? Throat so bronzed against the dark Lycra, face gleaming like silk from a run. His bright eyes roam over the whole property, from chimneys to the half-submerged windows of the cellars, from the modern wing, across the Victorian conservatory, to the elegant eighteenth-century proportions of the library windows.

He smiles, a broad smile. There's no-one around to smile at. He's smugly satisfied. Disturbing to watch. I know why, because I remember what he said after the library ceiling came down. One day Anthony Street-Langton intends to own the whole of Loughnian House.

Amy's wandering about like a sick dog. She's depressed about the studio, adrift of her normal life. 'I'll miss you, Charis,' she says. 'You're a sympathetic spirit.' I sense she feels there's a lack of the sympathetic pulling-together that a communal approach would have brought. Perhaps it's her means of having company without the commitment of a relationship. Now there's a threat they'll all go separate ways. She'll never again be in such a promising situation.

I've said goodbye to Adelaide and Grace, wondering whether I'll ever see them again. They may be relocated when I next visit Amy. They're economizing because of the threat of becoming homeless. 'We have root vegetable soup each day for lunch,' explains Grace. 'Unfortunately, after a time it ceases to be uplifting. You will think of us, Charis? Often, I hope.'

I see the last of the Street-Langtons from the hall window, as they get into their car. Anthony's jacket whirls round him as he circles round the bonnet. Even his clothes radiate their own vitality. Melissa wears dark glasses, though there's no sun. Just as she climbs into the car, she stretches her arms to the sky, rotating her face up. It's impossible to tell whether in pain or in ecstasy. A slip of paper blows out of the decorative snakeskin mini-rucksack thrown over her shoulder. As the car disappears I go outside to rescue the document which can only tell me more about this fascinating couple. It's a list, but not one for shopping.

Things I love best
Tea by the fire.
Walking in the snow.
Lying on the shore listening to the sea and the gulls.
My Gran's Sunday lunch. Pork, lamb and then beef, in that order.
Hot-water bottles.
Sleeping babies.
Making pastry at Gran's big pine table.
Baby gurgles.

Now outside, I hope Cob will see me and come out. The Philosopher's House stands sullen, amid the dirty, near-vanished snow. It glowers at the world as if daring it to come near. In sunshine the building can be elegant, serene, but under the low, colourless January sky it's grey-minded and scheming, not revealing the warmth within that's created by Grace and by Amy. It's a wounded house.

What will happen to it if Guy can't afford to live there? Will it become a hotel, a conference centre? It's not large enough for either of those. Nor quite big enough for a nursing home. More likely it will decay beyond rescue, and speculators will pull it down to make way for a dozen desirable houses, commuter distance from London. Or maybe Anthony will buy it? He would transform the Philosopher's House, beyond recognition. Swimming-pool, Pimm's parties, *en suite* guest rooms. Style would prevail. Anthony's style. Imposing Anthony, suffocating history, leaving no room for the past. Conversation would die.

What will happen to Milo?

Why have I thought this? Almost as if he's still around in the house. That's stupid. Why did I think *What will happen to Milo?*

No-one appears and I go inside again. There's only a short time before the cab arrives. I haven't said good-bye to Cob. It's up to him to find me. I should see Guy, I suppose, but I can hardly bear to look at him now. He's like King Lear, old, emasculated, nothing has come to nothing.

Outside, in the drive, Amy's standing beside the taxi-driver. I go to the conservatory to collect my suitcase, and the doorbell rings. My heart thumps. It's Cob.

He and I walk through to the hall. I feel sick this part of my life's ending.

Cob stops suddenly and grabs me by the sleeve. He says, 'Will you write to me?'

I stop scuttling to the door and stand perfectly still to let this sink in. I feel impossibly happy. I want to jump so high in the air my head will hit the ceiling. I want to cry. I want to be opening the envelope right this minute.

I have the presence of mind to mutter, 'Only if you write first.'

PART TWO

Chapter Nine

At my boarding-school, Rebecca Winthrop confides, 'I learned a lot from this waiter in Tenerife. That's where we spent Christmas. Tenerife. You should have seen the size of it.'

Tolly Greenhaugh, who never speaks to me normally, even though we share a study, catches me alone, and bursts into tears. 'I haven't had a period for seven weeks.'

I stroke her head, knowing this is not friendship. 'We'll think it through.' Tolly needs someone halfway between a mate and a stranger, to share with. Perhaps she dimly recognizes I will understand the state of uncertainty. I give her the last of my chocolate digestives.

The next day, Tolly tells Rebecca, 'I've come on. My god, what a relief.' She never mentions the good news to me. It's as if the incident never occurred. The confidence was never an act of friendship. Only convenience, easily forgotten.

It's *my* decision to be set apart from the others. It's better than believing they choose to ignore me. What I hate most is their dearth of kindness, the lack of warmth among them. They would rather gossip secretly than help each other. I would never confide in any of these girls. There is no *goodness* in the school, but plenty of moral rules. Instructions about what we can't do, meet boys, go to the pub, shorten our uniform skirts above the knee. We're cushioned by bars of restriction rather than comforting pillows of generosity.

In English, Miss Eales says, 'I think it's time, Charis, to be a little less *perceptive*, and a tad stronger on evidence. Cut the intuition. I don't think you'll ever get a question about Charlotte Brontë mutilating Mr Rochester to compensate for her own inadequacies.'

The spring term drags by, and I come to realize my real life, the time when I'm properly alive, is when I'm at the Philosopher's House. Even when I was with my mother I lived in a shadowland, always waiting for the next disaster. Here at boarding-school I'm only waiting to get away from these alien creatures, yearning to be back among people I love. I sit on my bed at night, hugging my knees and longing to see Amy's sanguine face, Grace's gladdening smile. Even Cob. Cob, who promised to write to me. I've got the picture that was his Christmas present up on the wall. Conveniently it reminds me both of him and Amy.

He does write eventually. Spells my name wrong. For some reason this hurts.

Dear Karis,

What a strange name. It wasn't so odd when you were here because I never called you by it. It's not so much I'm missing you or anything, but Amy is getting me to do all the work on the studio now she's chosen the colours. It would have been better if you were here to help. I've been painting solidly for five days and the smell's making me feel sick. I'm working hard at night on revision.

110

Sussex has offered me a place. B and two Cs. For philosophy. The course sounds cool. They're not asking for grades that I can't manage. Guy was horrid when I told him. He asked if Sussex was a converted poly or something, and was it by the sea? Then he said the only course worth doing was at Oxford, so I'd have to make the best of it. I want a better response from you.

I've got another coat of buttermilk to put on in the bedroom.

Your turn to write now. You said you would.

      Best wishes

        Cob

I read the letter three times when it arrives, and another twice this evening. A letter is more important than the spoken word. It's here for ever. Like Milo's diaries. The spoken word, if unrecorded, is lost except for living in the memory, and then perilously vulnerable to distortion, erosion and fading. I'm tempted to tell Rebecca and Tolly, to show them I'm attractive enough to get a letter from a boy. But I don't. The others read their letters out loud, and make fun of them. They might demand I read this out, then make fun of it because it's not romantic. It is to me. Precious. I won't have them laughing at Cob. I won't have them spoiling this source of pure white joy. At night, before I go to sleep, my eyes alternate between the letter tucked safely in a book, and the picture he framed which hangs now above my bed.

I wait two days to reply.

Dear Cob,

    Thank you for your letter. I didn't really think you'd write. Actually, my name begins with Ch.

As in charismatic. I don't blame you for not knowing. I wish I were back in the Philosopher's House. Not because of you or anything, but because school is so boring. I'm working quite hard because we've got the mocks next week.

Fantastic about Sussex. What's up with Guy, being so mean? He's not a very *good* man, is he? I've been offered a place at Durham. Three As. I'll never get the grades.

Camilla Smyllie, in the science stream, has been expelled for having cannabis.

Most of the girls here are fed up because we're not co-ed. They would have transferred to a school with boys for the sixth form but they're mostly too dim to get in anywhere else.

I'm trying to think of something amusing to tell you.

I've thought and I can't.

I hope you might write back to me.

> Best wishes
> Charis

This evening I get a shock. Miss Eales who's on house duty comes into our study and says in her brittle, disapproving voice that there's a telephone call for me. I run down the two flights of stairs, and all the way down the first flight I'm hoping it might be Cob. All the way down the second, I'm thinking it might be Amy.

In the event, it's my mother, who has never before phoned me at school.

'Darlingest little person, how are you?' she trills.

'What's wrong?'

'What do you mean, what's wrong? Why should there be anything wrong? Can't a mother phone her dearest child without an excuse?'

'Great. Lovely. I'm glad you have. Think about you a lot. Wish I was home so we could have our mugs of hot chocolate when you come back from the theatre.' That's my life really; small oases of comfort in a cold desert.

'Nick is such a sweetie. So macho. Makes me feel petite. I hope you'll meet him at Easter. Are you happy too, darling?'

'School is horrible. I'd come home tomorrow, if it wasn't for getting into university. When are you coming to see me?'

'Of course you don't want to leave such a lovely school. It will give you class. Eventually. Especially as Daddy is kind enough to keep paying. Why don't you ask *him* to visit you? I would come myself, but the play is going so well. *Much* more of a play than a panto. The standard of acting is amazing.'

'That's great.'

'Got to go. Nick's gone in the shower. Miss you dreadfully.'

The line goes dead before I can say goodbye. I lean my head against the wall behind the phone, and keep my eyes closed until I'm certain no tears have plopped out. It sounds as if Nick's moved in. It sounds as if Mum's at his disposal. It looks like another doomed relationship.

The time between the Christmas holiday and Easter passes as if I'm in limbo. Incidents in the school fill up the days, but they're as flotsam washed up on the tide, lingering a span, then swept away again into the deep memory of the sea.

Easter falls late this year, so we break up a good week before the big weekend. I pitch my hockey stick in the school lake because I never need touch it again. The day for team training is gone, for better or worse. It might be good for boys, but it brings out the worst in all of us, especially as we always get beaten. At our school we thirst too little for glory. Our minds are on other things. Even mine.

Two days previously Mum had phoned again.

'Darling. Nick has two weeks between shows and wants to take me to Majorca for an Easter break.'

'Sounds great.' The most wonderful thoughts are going through my head.

'How would you like a splendid two weeks more with Amy? I mean, only if you want, darling. I could give it all up for you, of course. I've got two new bikinis.'

'Use factor sixteen, Mum.' I hope the bikinis won't be the end of Nick. She's spread more than she thinks these last years.

She whispers, 'Charis darling. This may be it. What will be best for the both of us. You could have a father figure again.' Mum sounds as if she might cry. Where's she dragged up the altruistic element from? Anyway, her life is happening elsewhere now, and so will mine be.

I'm where I feel most comfortable. It's wonderful to be back at the Philosopher's House. All the talk is that the new tenant is moving into the studio *today*. It's a *He*. Guy's kept him under wraps, and no-one's spotted him coming to look at the apartment. Typically, Guy refuses to divulge any details, although Adelaide and Grace are pink with anticipation. Guy says he couldn't guess the age. Couldn't remember about his job. Possibly something to do with publishing. How could he judge a man's appearance? Stupid Guy. Wicked Guy, tormenting Amy and Grace and Adelaide.

*   *   *

114

'Quick,' says Amy. 'Go and see the studio before he turns up. Tell me what you think.'

The living-room, which was the studio, and before that a tack-room, is still, empty of life. Because the place is no longer full of Amy, I'm aware of its own character. This stable isn't like the rest of the house where great events which happened long ago still influence the air. There, considered ideas, finite and balanced thoughts seeped into the walls over the years, and still breathe out their presence, like dead flowers in pot-pourri. Only horses lived in this building. Perhaps it was because there were no people thinking beyond the hunt or grooming that Amy was free to create. Perhaps she will be still more free to paint in the open air, without even the history of horses hanging over her.

'Do you like it?'

I pull myself into the present, and look round at the yellow and white walls, the clean varnished boards, the maize Shaker rugs. In the middle of the floor stands a yellow and blue bowl. It's a watery blue, like the sea in springtime, with sunflowers splurged all over it. Only Amy would leave it solitary on the pine boards, challenging common sense, instead of tidily on a shelf. I want to laugh with the sunflowers, they're so happy, so innocent, so untainted by sorrow and disappointment. Unlike those who live in the main house. Unlike the Philosopher's House itself.

'I want the place to be full of sunshine. What do you think of the bowl? I wanted it myself so badly, but then I could see it in the studio. I put it in the middle of the floor. A heavy hint. I know only the right person will come to this place now. Someone who will love that bowl.'

'I *do* hope so, Amy.'

'I must rush out, Charis, while the light is right.

Painting *en plein air* is working a treat. The gallery has taken a couple again. They were a bit cautious, they think I might go off into something that would offend the clients' sense of discreet colour. Of course, I still have my optimistic eye. Enhanced colours. The public likes optimism on its walls.' Amy pops back through the door, 'Here comes Cob,' she says, and winks. What is she thinking about?

'Hello,' he says. 'I saw you come over.'

'Right.' How stupid we've nothing more interesting to say to each other. He's had his hair cut, but it's as waywardly tufted as ever. His face is even thinner, more gaunt, more blade-keen. At least his fingernails are clean.

'What you doing here then?'

'Seeing what Amy's been up to.'

'What *I've* been up to, you mean. It took ages.' Cob stands, embarrassed, not willing to admit he's approached me. Not wanting to be here, more like.

I cast round for conversation. 'At least we've got our university places.'

'Haven't got our grades yet, though.'

'No.'

'Don't know what I'll do if I fail. Got hardly any work done, with Guy driving me to get the apartment finished.'

'Expect you'll have to revise all this holiday.'

'Should think so.'

This is it then. Cob's giving me the push.

'Absolutely,' I say, all priggish. 'You should see the amount I've got to do as well.'

'Right.'

'Better get on then, I suppose.'

Cob nods, and walks out of the studio.

I sit on the floor next to the bowl, and a pale spring sun comes through the wide studio window. I mustn't get upset because anything Cob might have felt for me is evaporated. I must dwell on my blessings. One of which is being here at all. I'm deeply within the room. I close my eyes and listen to it. I try to identify what I sense. I feel quite apart from the rest of the house, where Guy and his philosopher weigh so heavily over everything in those elegant rooms. I'm apart from the quixotic antics of dearest Amy, from her yearning for love, her proximity to pain and from the Gothic romance of the conservatory. Away from the cloistered religion of Grace, from her servitude and her self-denial. I am free. There have been no great minds living in these rooms, no stain upon the air by way of a shaping intelligence. There's nothing to disturb or agitate.

All around me the light is coming into the room, from windows at either end, and bouncing off the white walls. I'm centred within the light of this world, yet know nothing. It's a revelation. I am responsible for everything I shall be. *Condemned* to be free. This air is clean and new, upon which some further story might be written. Ungoverned by past ideas. Everything that happens now must be written anew. What use is philosophy, or reason, or religion, when we must all live out our own sorrow? How should I *know* what I should do? What is left that we can rely upon to guide us?

About midday, Amy and I pop in for a cup of tea with Grace and Adelaide. I spotted them earlier when I went to the studio, their pale shadows lurking behind the kitchen curtain.

'Charis, dear child.' Grace totters across the kitchen. 'I've made shortbread petticoat tails in anticipation. For you of course, and possible others.'

'Pop the kettle on,' says Adelaide, who is taking a short rest on the sofa. 'We're eagerly anticipating our new neighbour, as you can imagine. Apprehensive that we left the choice to Guy, because with our kitchen window overlooking the courtyard and studio we don't want anyone disagreeable. However, we *should* have a man living there in these days of violence and civil disobedience.'

'He's in publishing,' Grace interrupts, 'at least, Guy *thinks* he's in publishing.'

'He'll be special,' Amy confides. 'Called by the sunflower bowl. Possibly a chime to match mine.'

'I'm looking for my very own chime right here,' says Adelaide. She waves a bunch of envelopes at us. 'I posted my advertisement last week. Three replies already.'

'Open them, dear.' Grace almost skips on the spot with excitement. The first is written on violet notepaper.

'It's from a woman,' shrieks Adelaide. She races through the page. 'Dis*gus*ting. She keeps on about anatomical bits I didn't know I've got.' She tears it up with her thumbs and forefingers only, as if not to contaminate the whole hand. 'I'll have to find a hand mirror later to check it out.' A bit late for such curiosity, really. She moves on to the second reply. The paper is pearly cream and textured.

'This is from? This is from *Xerxes*. I'll read it to you.

'"How refreshing to find a lady of culture and discernment writing in my favourite newspaper. I couldn't eat any more of my egg after I'd read it. Dear lady, let me commend myself to your company. I simply adore the theatre and eating out. I have a computer on which I record my assessment of each play and then compare it with that of the critics. I'm amazed how much they miss. For example, I've believed for years that Falstaff is really the Celtic King Arthur, but have I ever come across that perception?

No, I have not. I shall be interested to hear your opinion."

'There's *three* more pages of this. Grace dear, could you write him a pleasant little note, saying that regretfully the lady of culture and maturity must have been older than anyone realized, and has since passed away.'

Adelaide picks up the last envelope. No fancy notepaper this time.

'This is more the ticket. Listen.

'"Dear unknown number 125581

"It's all a lottery isn't it? How about an introductory knees-up, no commitment, no regrets, only the possibility of things coming together. Name your hostelry within a thirty-mile radius of Marble Arch."'

Adelaide slowly exhales. Here is common sense. Here is straightforwardness. Just Basildon Bond torn straight off the pad.

'A tad careless to leave the gummy end still sticking to the top of the paper.' She starts to tear it off, only to discover it's holding three sheets of paper together. Identical letters addressed to different numbers.

'Oh well,' says Adelaide, assigning that to the wastepaper basket as well. 'He'll get enough replies as it is.'

Amy wanders casually over to the window and shrieks, 'He's arrived. There's a van at the door.'

'We've missed him. Thanks to your stupid letters. He's already inside.' Grace is upset. 'I've been doing potatoes all morning so as to be on hand.'

Adelaide joins Grace and Amy at the window. 'We might as well see what his furniture's like.'

'Don't spy on the poor man,' says Amy.

'We'll sit down,' agrees Grace, but doesn't.

Adelaide crams herself deeper into the shadow of

the window as she sees the studio door open. 'Look. Look. Oh.'

'Oh dear,' says Grace. 'I *am* sorry. He's so *young*.'

I push in to see the man who's bought Amy's studio, the man who will fall in love with Amy, because of his affinity with the sunflower bowl. For heaven's sake, he's not *that* young. At least forty. I suppose that *is* young if you're about seventy, which Adelaide must be. He looks about the same age as Amy, fortyish on a good day. But that's as far as the good news goes, I'm afraid He's plain. *Plain* plain. Potato plain. Pudding plain. Baggy. Scruffy. Dull. He won't compare well with Henry, Amy's ex. Henry's tall, a bit of a clothes-hanger, and quite craggy. I can see the appeal of Henry, even if he is cold, and has odd ideas about what to do under a duvet. Perhaps this new man's got a great personality. Let's hope so.

Grace casts round for optimism. 'Guy must be happy now he's sold the studio. He can get his beloved ceiling done.'

'Don't get excited, dear. He's still got his electrics to sort, and I can't live with this plumbing for much longer. We're too closely allied to the sewers for comfort.' Adelaide opens the grandfather clock and hauls out a box of soft centres she's been hiding from herself, saving them for when she needed comfort.

Grace pats her sister absent-mindedly on the head and says, 'Never mind, dearest, I'll cook you a consoling dauphinoise. In time of sorrow carbohydrate is such a solace.' Presently she adds, 'It could augur well for you, Amy.' She closes her eyes and thinks about the possibilities.

'I doubt it.' Amy's almost coy. Her heavy lids close slowly, and open slightly wider than before. Her head minimally inclines to the left. Only the observant would be able to catch Amy's body language. 'He'll be a lovely person if he liked the sunflower bowl.' She looks ridiculously optimistic. I'm wondering if Amy is short-sighted.

Adelaide says, 'I knew I should have been there to advise Guy.'

Later, Amy says, 'Someone ought to take him a drink. A symbol of welcome. We're a community after all. Notice I didn't say commune. Guy won't think about that, will he? You come *with* me.' Amy wipes Vaseline on her coarse lips as an afterthought, and rubs them together to work it in. They don't look any different. They retain their pachydermal quality. 'Should I take him a *pot* of tea?'

'The teapot lid's chipped.'

'A mug, then. Less pretentious than a whole pot.'

'Exactly right.'

'We won't linger while he drinks it. Don't want to appear over-interested. Anyway, he'll have to bring the mug back.' She giggles happily. When Amy giggles it's only the sound you get, a soft, bubbling noise coming from the region of her tonsils, but no shifting of the features.

We arrive at the studio as the man returns from his car with several carriers. Plastic bags never make for elegance, especially when they're from a *sava* type of supermarket, and with contents spewing out. The sleeve of a red sweater trails from one, catching the floor. A spider plant burgeons from the top corner of another. I hope Amy won't say anything silly like *Oi* or *excuse me*. He goes in and closes the door, unaware of our eyes piercing the back of his head. Amy carefully carries before her the china mug, already having managed to slop tea over the side in an unbecoming smear. She knocks tentatively.

The door lurches open, ricocheting back on its

hinges. The great personality on which I'm pinning my hopes isn't in evidence yet. His untucked shirt hangs like limp laundry over shapeless faded blue shorts. He carries a bowl with DOG written on the side, and a can of pet food. Bare feet sprout huge big toes, upturned and aggressive. I understand big noses have implications, but I don't know about big toes. Such sex signals are too sophisticated for someone who's never even been kissed. Would Amy know?

She smiles. He's very lucky. Her eyes beam out warmth in that special way, her mouth parts slightly, not exactly curling up. It's a very good smile. For her, that is. 'Welcome. I'm Amy. This is Charis. Thought you might need some coffee. Though it's tea actually.' Amy comes near to a silly giggle. 'Moving home is one of the three most stressful things in life.'

'Is it?' He stares out as if his eyes are opaque, and he doesn't register us. There's no indication of lust when he sees my aunt for the first time. Not even a hint.

He holds his hand out for the mug, nods. That's as far as he goes towards thanking Amy for her consideration.

Amy is undeterred. '*I* designed the studio.' She lets this sink in for a moment, but gets no response. 'I hope everything is to your liking?'

'It'll do me.' This is the longest sentence so far. Three words instead of two. Enough to detect the Welsh accent. That's the end then. I remember Amy has a low opinion of the Celts to the west.

'Excellent. Well, I suppose we must be going.' Amy hovers a moment longer, waiting for the invitation to step inside. I glance into the room, and see the sunflower bowl. It's shoved almost out of sight on the top shelf of his ceiling-high bookcase. *Not* appreciated. Fortunately Amy doesn't look beyond the door. She's not one for spying. She closely observes only what she wants to paint.

'Thanks for the drink,' he says at last. Four words this time. He's coming on.

'You're welcome. I didn't catch your name.'

'Because I didn't say it. Laurie.'

I can't help thinking it's more Lorry as in vehicle, than Laurie in *Little Women*.

'Lovely,' says Amy, mindlessly. 'Cheerio then, Laurie.'

'He's not got two heads,' I point out as we walk home. 'There's a load of books so he can't be stupid.'

'I shouldn't get your hopes up, Charis.' Amy speaks lightly, but I sense disappointment. Amy admires vitality. It's what Henry had. Vitality. Too much vitality, as it happens. That was the problem.

Chapter Ten

For lunch we have salami and chutney sandwiches. Amy, sated, so more optimistic, says, 'Quite an interesting man, Laurie.' Having rejected unfortunate first impressions, she's planning what to say when he comes back with her tea mug. 'I wonder what he does. A writer, do you think? Freelance journalist, perhaps. A temperament sympathetic to my own.'

Melissa knocks on the window, peering through the conservatory glass. 'Laurie asked me to return your mug,' she calls.

Amy strives to look grateful, and lets her in. 'Right. Thanks.'

'I popped round myself with coffee. Seemed the thing to do.' She's languid in a soft damson suede dress. It hangs like silk. She didn't get *that* in a chain store. I'm thinking she doesn't have a reason, like Amy does, for visiting Laurie. Well, I hope not.

'What a beautiful conservatory.' Melissa's breathless with admiration. 'I'd love a garden room like this.' She pats the cushion with the cross-eyed pigeon, strokes the abutilon flowers. 'I feel an empathy.' She speaks the word as if it were a perfume. The conservatory takes on a golden light.

'Anthony could buy you one,' says Amy.

'This is old. It was a different life then, wasn't it? Things were settled. I like that feeling. You don't get it in our kitchen. It's too new. I like a comfy kitchen.'

'Yes,' says Amy. She notices Laurie hasn't washed her mug.

'He runs a press-cuttings agency. Guy told me that.' Melissa feels some explanation is necessary, as if knowing the nature of Laurie's work is an introduction. She adds, 'He's split up from his woman because she wanted more commitment.'

That's some relief. He's not against women. And he's without at the moment.

'You know a great deal,' says Amy. I recognize coldness in her voice. Amy is not pleased.

'After the coffee we shifted things round in the shed to accommodate his car. Guy moved the Rover over, and Anthony had stored boxes there. I had to move them against the wall.' She smiles, displaying her even and slightly backward-slanted teeth. Teeth that go with fresh breath. 'Ever so easy to get on with.'

'I see,' says Amy, who doesn't.

Melissa's eager to share. 'He'll have to leave for work every morning at eight o'clock. St Albans. That's where his press-cutting office is. Will get back at half-past six. There's time to take the dog a walk before he goes.'

'Something rather lonely about living with a dog,' says Amy. 'As if you can't quite make it on your own.' She's not forgiven Laurie for failing to return the mug personally.

'The woman was called Megan.'

'The Welsh are very devious,' says Amy. The points against Laurie are piling up. 'Are you *still* making room in the garage?' she asks with heavy sarcasm.

'He has a home computer. Plays chess on it.' Melissa is impressed.

'No worse than auto-eroticism, I suppose.'

'The dog's called Rufus.'

'Bloody hell,' says Amy. 'You've got to admire his imagination.'

Melissa stares at me. 'You've still got your school look,' she says. I think she means I'm looking very plain. I'm right, because she says next, 'You looked so pretty at Christmas in that green top.'

'Oh well,' I say, meaning that it's one thing for *her* to talk like that. I'm made this way.

'Eye-shadow,' says Melissa. 'If there's one thing I do know it's eye-shadow. Come back with me, and I'll sort some out.' Here's another bit of style I'm going to borrow. A magpie, that's what I am.

Melissa's back door is locked, so we go all round the house past Guy's library to get in at the front, and, on the way, spot Grace in her herb garden.

She kneels on a mat covered in red and white gingham, with a trowel in one hand and a box of plants beside her, harmonious with the herb garden begun centuries ago by the nuns. She wears a sun-bonnet, nursery-rhyme style with fabric gathered at the back to shade her neck. Grace doesn't look surprised to see us.

Melissa stands like a lofty angel beside the kneeling Virgin. Grace hands her a bunch of herbs, almost as if she's picked them ready to give. 'Put them in boiling water and treat it like tea. An infusion,' says Grace. 'Lady's mantle and yarrow. It may taste bitter.'

Melissa's puzzled. 'What's this for?'

'Seems the best thing to do.' There's a question in Grace's eyes.

'Thank you,' Melissa says, and walks away frowning. Completely forgets my eye-shadow lesson.

I lean forward and kiss Grace's cheek, dry to the touch, like an autumn leaf. Her mottled brown hands clutch mine. I'm enveloped in the smell of lily of the valley. It's sharp and fresh. Springlike. Not autumnal, as she is.

She pats the grass beside her. 'Camomile,' she says. 'Rather obvious. I'm not an original woman. The herbs sprout from wedges of soil, the intervals of a clock, perennials well on their way, others still lime-pale seedlings. Looming at the centre, a stone St Francis of Assisi, a bird on one shoulder and a squirrel running up his arm. He's of light stone, but plastered with what appears to be face cream and chocolate.

'I'm ageing it,' Grace says. 'Yoghurt and compost. I once went to a country house where they did all their urns that way. Should be dung but we have none to hand. I improvised.'

She kneels as if she were in a pew, symmetrical, back upright, only her head low. Planting as a form of prayer. Leaning forward, she picks me a sprig. 'Comfrey to heal wounds.'

'Am I wounded?'

'Demonstrating what I have. Feverfew for headache. Horseradish for aching feet. Calendula for my own age spots.'

Grace has found her home, the setting in which she could become a jewel. 'It's strange, Charis, when I'm among my herbs I see more. I see into the heart of things. I find it easier to pray.'

'You're always praying, Grace. Do you get what you want?' Nothing exciting ever happens to Grace.

'I don't know, Charis. I don't pray for myself, and if I ask for someone else's happiness, I can never be sure they receive. People are extraordinarily ungrateful. Not to me, I don't expect anything. Anyway, they don't know of my interventions. But ungrateful to God. For life. For just looking happy.'

'Who isn't grateful?'

127

'Guy for one. I've prayed so hard for that man to be happy. You'd think he'd try.'

'Perhaps he doesn't want to be happy.'

'You may have something there, dear. His childhood's to blame. In my childhood they tried to put me *down*. Quite the opposite with Guy. I didn't know him as a child of course, but from little things he's said over the years. His father expected too much of him. He wanted Guy to be a scholar and an athlete at school, then be either a barrister or the Prime Minister. Rather a tall order. A jury would be quite bowled over by him, of course. But I think he'd have lost his temper with the House of Commons. Of course, he did neither and finishes up thinking he's a failure. Perhaps you're right. I shouldn't expect Guy to be happy.'

'What's your latest project?'

'Not project. Too businesslike a word. I'm not at all certain I should have done it anyway. Might amount to interference.'

'*What*, Grace?'

'For Amy. This Laurie. For poor Amy. So wild. So lost. And pagan. I'm afraid God might be losing patience with her. But if she were to be happy? Who knows? Is it for me to explain all this to the Almighty? I'm afraid it's not. Not my place at all.'

If there is a god, he'd surely look after Amy if he looked after anyone. She's definitely in the lost-sheep class. Amy wouldn't travel with the herd at any cost, and woolly she'll always be. The Gospels make it clear God has a special affinity with the ovine genus. 'Perhaps you should leave it to him,' I say weakly. Sort of acknowledging Grace's caring, and her god's overwhelming love at the same time. I'm a hypocrite.

'It's an eternal problem isn't it? Knowing whether one is expected to point out little deficiencies.' Grace levers herself to her feet and wanders off indecisively into the house. I'm always being abandoned.

Amy's painting in the garden. *En plein air*. It's the next day. She has a couple of sweaters on under her smock, so she doesn't look any slimmer. I'm glad Laurie is likely to be out of the way, at his office. Guy comes round the corner of the house, scowling as usual.

'The price of the studio won't cover the ceiling, the wiring *and* the plumbing,' he says accusingly. 'I had to lower the price to sell at all. Put it down to your garish décor. Roses on trellises is what we should have had. To attract the affluent widow with rural inclinations. But you had to know best.'

'I *do* know best,' says Amy, calmly. 'Which is why I have my interim idea.'

'If it's like the rest of what comes out of that puerile pocket you call your brain I don't want to hear it.' Guy sounds even crosser than he did at Christmas. I expect he's not got over Milo having a love life. Being human instead of a genius.

'It's *better*,' says Amy, not in the slightest put out.

Guy walks to the end of the terrace, his hands behind his back, indecision looming around him like a fairy cloak. He turns round. Amy measures up the height of a tree by squinting at a paintbrush at arm's length, as artists like to do.

'What is it then?' Guy shouts across the terrace.

Amy minimally cocks her head to make him come within normal speaking distance. 'We'll open the house to the public on Easter Sunday. Advert in the local paper. Notice on the door of the village shop. The gardens are looking good. Grace has put in loads of work. Not quite the Lost Gardens of Heligan, but on the same lines. I doubt *they've* got an abbey herb garden. Your library is almost as it always was, apart from the ornate bits on the ceiling. All the genuine dust back in place.'

'That's typical of the woman you are. A ridiculous idea. A couple of weeds and a stick of rhubarb don't constitute a herb garden. The village will come all right. Nosy bastards. Want to gloat over the great house sinking into decay. You bet they do. Sneering. Laughing. Then go home to their nasty little mortgaged terraces with plastic urns and French marigolds, and *talk* about me. The last thing we need is half the bloody village trampling over everything.'

'Half the village would be a waste of time,' agrees Amy. 'How many people do you think see this house from the road and fancy a squint round? See the man who owns it all? To the outside world, you're an intriguing character.' I spot, but Guy doesn't, the flicker of a smile cross her face. Guy does have, I imagine, the reputation of being a *genuine* eccentric, an increasingly endangered species at this time of uniform and assiduously cultivated idiosyncrasy.

'I don't want people here staring at me, you stupid woman.'

'Admiring the glory of it all. Ancestry going back all that way. There's nothing like envy to make people nosy.'

'Ancestry I have. Glory there once was. Glory hangs on among the ruins perhaps, like it does in Greece. Envy, you suppose?' Guy cocks his head like a hopeful thrush listening for a worm. 'Do you think I'm still hung around with a remnant of glory?'

'It's there in your bones, Guy. Class. Breeding. Blood.'

'I suppose a few bob on account wouldn't come amiss.'

'We'll have a meeting. Settle it either way,' says Amy, not yet making the final push for this communal effort. She's playing him like a fish on a line.

'I expect it might surprise some of the rank and file,' Guy muses.

'They'll be covetous. Jealous as hell.'

'You have my permission to organize the meeting, Amy. Tonight after dinner.'

'*You* can organize it,' replies Amy, unmoved. 'At my place. To suit when you've washed up your baked-bean saucepan.'

Chapter Eleven

'Ladies and er . . . gentle*man*,' says Guy. 'I have called you together. Reluctantly. Cost of the ceiling still looms. Electrics. Drains. If I sink, you sink with me.' He leers threateningly. 'Project Studio Flat has not yielded total solution. An interim measure has been suggested. A small, insignificant operation. Might cover the cost of a few plugs.'

Amy sits cross-legged on her sofa, like a tranquil Indian local deity, emanating calm and detachment from Guy's anxiety. From beneath the striped damask letters and newspapers peep out, like inquisitive mice. A smile, little more than fleeting, hangs on her heavy lips. We're operating as a commune. We're thinking collectively on a common project. Amy's slightly sorry that Laurie isn't yet sufficiently integrated to be invited to the meeting. She nods minimally at Guy to encourage his bumbling explanation.

Guy's a mix of embarrassment and authority. He doesn't approve of what he's suggesting, but thousands of years of upper class leadership is coming through.

'Amy has come up with the crazy notion of opening us to the public. Easter Sunday.'

He's all smiles once he's delivered the threat, the blackmail bit. Adelaide beams back, her ample frontage heaving up and down with excitement. She thinks she's dowager material.

Grace puts her hand up tentatively, as if she's in school and only half knows the answer. She stands up and warbles, 'I could do cakes,' then collapses back down into her chair. The chair wouldn't tolerate that from Adelaide.

Anthony, leaning fastidiously against a wardrobe stencilled with butterflies that Amy currently happens to have in her sitting-room, sneers, 'Do you think a library and a few cakes might be a bit *thin*?'

Guy's aristocratic authority is wasted on him. Guy's money is only *inherited*, he's thinking. Anthony must be richer than Guy through his own endeavours. Gambling in the money markets takes a quick mind. Anthony believes it takes brains. He adds, 'Scarcely worth the punters' fifty pees.'

Amy stands up, looking shorter than ever without her shoes. 'I volunteer this drawing-room,' she says magnificently. 'And my kitchen. By that, I mean the conservatory. I'll have to shift my gear. Conservatories are what they're all into these days.' Amy is certainly giving her all for the sake of this community.

Anthony lets his eyes glide round the room with mock horror. 'I suppose you want my dining-room next?'

Guy ignores the sarcasm. 'That's remarkably good of you, Anthony. I'll check with your good lady.' He lifts an already lofty eyebrow towards Melissa.

She looks pale and in Rossetti mode, with her hair falling thick around her. She's wearing a long slim black silk coat, with the collar pulled up. What I most admire is how she has so many guises. 'Of course,' she says, demure as a nun. She glances at Anthony, unsmiling. I sense a score.

'I can't get everything in the bedroom,' says Amy,

having volunteered her rooms before she'd thought out the consequences.

'There's room in the shed where I keep the Rover,' says Guy grudgingly. 'It may necessitate you keeping your little motor outside, Anthony.'

'I'll personally conduct the visitors round. I empathize with the ladies of the National Trust,' says Adelaide. 'They're classily impoverished. That's why they do it.'

'I was hoping to persuade Mrs Street-Langton,' says Guy rather shyly. 'Make us look a bit more vogue and all that.'

'I beg your pardon,' says Adelaide. 'Education is *the* key element. I have a school certificate in history.'

'What's a school certificate?' Melissa asks.

Adelaide bounces from the room in a huff, and trips over something outside.

'Bugger,' she says, her voice no longer low and throaty. I go out to see if she's broken her leg. She's built to fall heavily.

She's hauling herself to her feet, panting gustily. On the floor, on all fours, is Laurie.

'What the hell are you playing at?' Adelaide demands.

'Keep still everyone,' he says. There is slight panic in his Welsh voice, making it rise.

Laurie looks straight at me, unfocused as he was yesterday. 'My contact lenses,' he says. 'I've come to tell Guy there's hot water coming out of the cold tap. Half-way across the hall I sneeze, and they jump out. I lost them yesterday as well. In the move.'

Slowly he crawls forward, his face close to the carpet, feeling the greasy pile with his fingers. I hope he doesn't have a delicate nose. The heel of his left shoe slips down and there's a hole in his sock. Quite a large one. Amy brings a torch, and eventually we find the lenses winking among the dust.

'Wonderful,' says Laurie, cleans them with a lick, and turns his back on us while he refits his eyes. He wheels round, and something extraordinary happens. Laurie is transformed. The consequence is profound. He no longer ignores us, but focuses firmly on each of us in turn. He beams on me, and I see he's got extra-ordinary eyes. They're blue-green, with olive-brown segments, like dirty river water in the sunlight. They're caring and warm and unfathomable.

He was cold and aloof yesterday because he couldn't see anything properly. Now Amy's come into focus, and he's looking at her for the first time. Seeing her anew. He's taking a long look. Face starts to crack into a smile. He's not as ancient as I'd supposed. Nor as potato-like.

'You're Amy,' he says and holds out his hand. 'Thank you for the tea. I couldn't come round to thank you until I found my lenses, you see.' He seems to for-get I'm there. She's fallen into the intimacy of his vision, a clear face instead of a featureless head. He's reoriented, and Amy is revalued.

'No problem,' she says and smiles. So extensively she shows her teeth.

'Work to be done,' says Guy, the next morning. 'We should employ a duster. Round the books. Woodprints. Charis, a job for you. Local hillsides and duckponds and other mundane sights. Used to hang in the hall. Took them down when we became apartmentized. The hall was too public for their good. I know the tenants better now. More or less trustworthy. Prints must be somewhere in the attic. Make a world of difference to that hallway. For the public, you understand. I begin to warm to the unwashed masses.'

'Want some help?' Cob asks, with the briefest glance at me.

'I want *you* to tidy the forsythia on the drive,' says Guy, 'and I want it done by lunchtime.'

Cob shrugs his shoulders, and apologizes to me with a one-sided smile. Please be like this more often Cob, I think, instead of so cocky and knowing. I dare to say as I pass him, 'It may take me until the afternoon.' Immediately, I feel a blush coming on. What sort of invitation will he think that is? I just don't know the right things to say. I scurry away.

It takes two hours' searching on the top floor to locate the wretched woodprints. All the rooms up here are given over to storage, not just those at the top of Guy's servant stairs, but those near the main staircase as well. It's difficult because everything is covered, either in sheets or black plastic. Guy hasn't told me where to look. I keep thinking about the stupid remark I made to Cob. I *must* be out of here by the end of the morning. Before he's finished the forsythia.

I locate the pictures, wrapped in brown paper, only daring to undo corners for fear of exposing valuables to mice and polluting dust. The prints are Victorian and sombre, the first two are hunting scenes. Amy won't be keen on these. Perhaps blood sports could go on the upstairs landing. The rest are a variety of remarkably heavy ducks perched on various mud-flats. Ducks look pessimistic if they're not bobbing merrily on water.

I secure three under each arm, and decide to use the front stairs because they're less steep. Between the first and second floors, the stairs change direction twice, so the whole flight isn't visible at one time. From round the bend comes an unexpected sound. Like a sack being dragged along.

Perhaps it's Cob. Big panic. But it can't be. There's a muffled scuffling, then groaning. Something's on the first turn, perhaps approaching the second. I could go down and confront whatever it is, but I don't. For all the strangeness, I'm not frightened. There's no menace. If necessary, I can retreat into the room and pile cases up against the door. Even escape down the back stairs. I wait. More of the same grunts.

Round the corner of the stairs comes a hand, a wrinkled, old hand. Then another. Then the arms. Grace hauls herself into view. With closed eyes, she is heaving herself up the stairs by her elbows. Now she's on the last flight, with laboured breathing, she keeps stopping. She mutters, 'Dear God forgive me. Forgive your faithful servant for I have presumed. Please. Please. Only forgive.'

I step back into the box-room and stay still. Grace is doing penance. Like pilgrims crawling up two hundred stone steps at Rocamadour to get to the church with the miraculous black Virgin. We once went there, while camping in France with a particularly fit and hearty uncle. The penance must be for daring to instruct God what to do about Amy. Grace would be mortified, if she knows I've seen her. This is private. I would step further back into the room, but I might make a noise. The best I can do is freeze.

Grace has further instructions. As her hands reach the top step, she whispers, 'Dear God. Take these carnal longings from me. Let me forget him. Make me not to dream.' She pulls herself up, turns and sits, exhausted, on the top step, back against the newel post. Then she crosses her arms, grasping each shoulder, cradling herself. Gently, she drops her head and kisses the back of her left hand. She drops her arms, and stares unseeing down at the wooden step. She half smiles and whispers, 'My dear one. Go from my mind. Leave me in peace.'

Slowly she stands up and walks down the stairs quite normally. I hang around until I'm certain she's cleared the landing.

Chapter Twelve

By Easter Sunday the word is round that cantankerous Mr Loughnian is on view up at Loughnian House, and if anyone wants to see how the old crank lives, now is their chance. Since relatives visit on Easter Sunday and have to be entertained, it looks as if there'll be a good turnout for our open day.

Grace is upset she can't make fresh cakes in the morning as she'll be at her devotions. Easter's top of her calendar. She's asked Amy to take charge of the baking, which is not a wise move, as Amy has never quite sussed the Aga for cakes. If anything edible emerges, and the day is warm, we plan to serve tea on the terrace. Unfortunately, it turns out to be cold, though dry, so everyone has to cram into the hall for their eats. Not the most elegant setting, although we've inadvisedly hoovered the carpet. The vacuum devoured several clumps of thread, so the floor looks more stressed than ever. The hall it has to be. We need the limited selection of other rooms for viewing, not for eating in.

In the event, Amy's sponges are of uneven colour and height, and unequal density. Runny jam smudges out of the seams. When sliced, there's a tendency to collapse. The scones, in contrast, are robust and resistant to the knife. Grace, though still mellow from church, shudders at the sight of them.

We have a guide posted in each room to restrain pilfering, even though Guy's removed all portable vases and statuettes that might tempt those he identifies as the bottom strata of society. Adelaide stands menacingly in the centre of the library, ready to instruct. Melissa wafts between Amy's drawing-room and the conservatory, lending class. Anthony says he'll look after the dining-room, but he's deep into his mobile phone in the garage. I'm on the gate, and we're asking one pound, including for children, as Guy wants to discourage undisciplined offspring, possibly not house-trained. Cob will watch out for anything untoward in the grounds. The village is an unknown quantity socially to most of those who live in the Philosopher's House. Guy's suspicions tend to be infectious.

Anthony, never known to garden, lights a bonfire, and its smoke drifts over the herb garden. I wonder why he so begrudges this effort to save Guy's home.

Cob joins me at the gate to scrutinize all who come through. There's been a steady flow since mid morning. Perhaps we should have done lunches. No, not without Grace. From time to time Cob turns back to the house to check no-one's picking the narcissi. He slides his back down one of the pillars of the gatepost and sits with his arms crossed, staring down to the village, the church at the centre.

Surprisingly, he smiles up at me. 'I keep wondering about Milo's grave. With it being on the edge, and yet the space was extended more recently, it looks as if he wasn't buried in the churchyard originally.'

'What does that mean?'

Cob shrugs. 'Your guess is as good as mine.' His

139

angular brows are quizzical. There's something he's not telling me. I refuse to give way to curiosity. Instead I make my own contribution.

'Do you think there's a ghost here?'

'Of course not. Only a girl would think that.'

'When I'm in parts of the house. With the old furniture. I get this funny feeling. I did at Christmas.'

'This funny feeling? *This* funny feeling? Loose use of language, Charis. I thought English was one of your As.'

'And History.' I try to channel my priority interests.

'Then ghosts will come in admirably.'

I don't like this cocky Cob, arrogant as he was the day I met him. He's moved towards me since then, and shown he's vulnerable. Now he's moving away again. Sussex is claiming him already.

A woman walks out of the gate. Her handbag is sprouting coriander leaves.

'She's been nicking Grace's herbs,' says Cob.

'Grace won't begrudge them. She'll say that it's all healing.'

'People like Grace do inestimable harm to the intellectual growth of this country,' says Cob.

'Grace could never harm anyone.'

'The revelation of God. It's a fire-blanket on the flame of philosophy.'

'What will you do when you've got a degree? Banish all religions?'

'Set up a course for schools. Insist it's part of the core curriculum. Necessary for what the clerics call DIY morality. They look down their noses, think men still listen to them. They don't realize people *must* think for themselves. It's called Individualism. Happened before. With the Greeks, then during the Renaissance. And of course, the Enlightenment. This time it must be different.'

'Because it's you?' I'm beginning to sneer myself.

'No. Different because in the past only educated men realized the importance of the individual. Then Mrs Thatcher said *everyone* could be an individual. Problem was, she forgot all about schools. Freedom without education is anarchy. There was no leap forward for civilization with her. We just got to have more belongings.'

'Very clever. Neat. Why do you have to go on as if you know all the answers?' I'm cross because that's exactly what I was thinking in Amy's studio, the morning before Laurie moved in. But I couldn't put it into words. There's got to be more than just having *freedom*. 'Are you sure it's *education* that's needed?' I feel it's down to something else that I can't put my finger on.

'I do know the answers. We're responsible for ourselves. Philosophy alone gives us the means to know what we should do.' He's like he was the first time I saw him. Prickly. Defensive. The angles of his eyebrows and mouth are like shafts across his face, armour against being diminished. Weapons against *me*.

He senses my antagonism. 'I'll look after the gate if you like.' This is his way of dismissing me. I walk back to the house feeling hurt and excluded. Cross with myself for not arguing my corner. Why do we try to talk when we get on so badly? Why does Cob have to be all head and no heart?

In the hall Amy dispenses wedges of coffee cake with a slice. Where the butter icing oozes out, she tries to wipe it off, but only smears it over the top, further limiting the visual appeal. Laurie helps Amy hand round cake. He drops the first plate, and the sponge spreads out over the floor, mousse-like. 'Liquid cake,' he says. 'What an amazing woman. I've never met a woman before who can make amorphous cakes.'

Amy doesn't quite know how to take this, but eventually giggles. We glimpse her teeth again. 'What can the women you meet usually do?'

'A lot of them sing,' says Laurie, as if having a problem recalling. 'At least Megan did. We were both in the choir. St Enedoc's. She was chapel at heart, she only went to the English because of the choir. I went because the repertoire was extensive. It wasn't so much that her soprano was on the squeaky side that I saw the light, more the pleasures she denied herself on a Sunday. I mean, Sunday morning's a good time, isn't it?'

'Would you prefer herb tea?' Grace asks.

I climb the stairs and look down on the activity from above. The middle landing is quiet, Grace and Adelaide's apartment empty. What a beautiful house this once was when properly lived in. From the first-floor landing window I see the landscape spread out, rich ploughed land, a hint of spring corn, grazing sheep. All of this once belonged to the Loughnian family. Here, within the walls, would have been living flames in all the fireplaces against the cold of the world, laughing and gossip in each room, bustle and life among the servants. While this house stands, something of those people can still linger, still matter. Be remembered. By us. If the house deteriorates, finally demolished, they too will be gone, along with this part of our own lives.

There's a stratum of silence above the chink of cups below, the babbling, grumbles, the shuffle of feet. In that silence I sense a quiet laughter, an amused chuckle. I have the weirdest sensation that the Philosopher is laughing at what we're doing here today. I don't expect to *see* a ghost. He's one more thing

I feel under my eyelids. Reluctantly, I return down-stairs to see if I can help.

Melissa, her hair in a pony-tail, wafts among those inspecting Amy's drawing-room and conservatory. She clasps her hands, repeating, 'Isn't it all lovely?' She infects the village with her smile. Some of them try out the sofa. They touch the Aga. They stroke the plants. I wish they weren't here, gawping at Amy's belongings.

Adelaide's in the library, being dynamic. She's gild-ing the lily. 'Here the dreaded Mortmain killed his wife when he discovered her *in flagrante delicto*. Poor Lady Lilian still walks the upper gallery at night. I've heard her footsteps myself.'

'Shall we see the upper gallery?'

'I'm afraid that is not on our itinerary today.'

'Would this be after the Philosopher or before?' A man in a flat hat looks suspicious.

'We're unable to establish the details. Vital papers were destroyed. We have only our dear little ghost to go by.' Adelaide smiles beguilingly, as if she's just pro-duced a rabbit. Her voice is throatier than ever. She stands square, difficult to argue against.

At this moment there's a creaking behind her, and the sash-frame glides down, the window closing itself. Weird. I expect the sash-cord's going. Another expense for Guy.

'Ah,' says Adelaide, thinking quickly. 'Lady Lilian is feeling the draught. That will do, dear lady.' She smiles triumphantly.

A small child breaks loose and pushes aside the cur-tain with a view to swinging on it, untouched by the possibility of a murky Lady Lilian hidden there. The nearest we come to seeing a spirit is the glass of sherry Adelaide's secreted there, to fortify herself against men in flat hats with searching questions. She catches the child on the last swallow, and snatches back the glass, too late. 'I hope you get alcoholic poisoning you thieving little cretin.'

The child runs away screaming and Grace, coming in from the hall, unable any longer to look at Amy's dysfunctional cakes, gathers it up in her arms. Its tears smear her neck, and an expression of joy crosses her face. She's no longer a barren woman. She must notice the sherry fumes emanating, but she stares down at the child in wonder. From its place of safety, the child puts out its tongue at Adelaide. The man in the flat hat tries to wrest it off Grace.

I see that the sash-cords are still intact. I wonder if Cob has arranged this little display, and look outside. He can't have done. He's only now walking up from the main gate. A smile creeps up on my face. Not so much *my* smile, as a borrowed smile. I think Milo Loughnian may be doing his bit to keep the house interesting. I hear that chuckle again, deep inside my ear.

Guy, strangely overcome by modesty, has been skulking elsewhere, to avoid staring eyes. Possibly because he fancies some cake, he now appears at the door. He approaches the child with a view to endearing himself to its parents. 'What a splendid little fellow to come and see us.' He playfully taps the child on its head and gets a whiff of the sherry. The boy burps, mouth wide.

'That child's drunk,' Guy barks. 'Intoxicated. We should alert the social services.'

Flat hat is now in possession of his offspring. 'I shouldn't bother,' he says nastily, 'until after we've got the white coats in for the rest of you. Bossy boots strutting her stuff in here. Some gormless dream in the other room. That poncy fellow in shiny shoes with his mobile, smoking the place out with a bonfire. Food that wouldn't pass the kitchen safety regulations.'

'Tea's in the hall, Guy.' Adelaide is firm. She turns to the visitors. 'It's such fun having an eccentric like Guy in our midst. We all need colour in our lives.' She smiles menacingly at him, and tries to use one eyebrow to indicate the hall. 'Coffee cake, Guy.'

Guy fixes each one in turn, including Adelaide. 'Anything missing, and I'll know where to look.'

'Now, now, Guy, you don't mean that,' says Adelaide. Grace is smiling benignly at the child, hoping he'll smile back.

'Come along Wayne,' says flat hat. 'Never get into a car with anyone like these people here.'

'Knew there was something funny up here,' agrees a man with braces over his vest. More rumbles from others. There's a general drift towards the front door.

Our visitors melt away, with backward glances at the master of the house. Satisfied they were right to be wary.

Gone is our chance to make money by opening the Philosopher's House to the public. A forfeited opportunity to pay for even some small part of Guy's destructive, ever-encroaching precipice of debt.

Chapter Thirteen

After Amy's less than impressive performance with the cakes, I take over the catering. Amy isn't interested in food. On Tuesday the village shop is open again and I make the best of its shineless tomatoes and sweating carrots. Cob catches me up at the gate of the Philosopher's House. He's been weeding the shrubbery. Hope he's in a better mood than he was on Sunday afternoon.

'Hello.' He takes the carrier bag from me. Such a gallant gesture makes my inside turn over. No-one's done that before. Carried my bags. It's personal. It wouldn't be his natural manners. At my school, it's a big thing if one of the boys from the village offers to carry the library books. I think about what's supposed to happen next. With that lot it's usually hotfoot to the back of the hockey pavilion. Well on the way for the *Ultimate Experience*. I'm not ready for that today. Anyway, Cob won't be interested in me for any of the right reasons. I mustn't be stupid.

We have the whole of the drive to walk up. Bliss.

'Guy's told me he'd sell my cottage, but he doubts I'll stick the philosophy course.'

'Considering Guy's into philosophical ethics himself, he's pretty nasty.'

Cob's face splinters into a grin. It's a lovely smile. The sharp angles dissolve. He looks attractive.

'Did you get those other letters deciphered?' I ask. 'Milo's letters in the box.'

'No,' he says vaguely. 'There was so much to do in the studio. Now there's revision.' He doesn't look me in the face.

'But you were so excited to find them.'

Cob shrugs. 'Anyway Guy doesn't deserve to know about them. He's always sniping at me.'

Perhaps because he's carrying my shopping, perhaps because he's told me about Guy, I lose some of my stupid inhibitions. 'He's not a kind man.' Lightly I touch his arm, just above the wrist. Only for a second. It's quite damp.

For me, that's *intimate*.

Amy says, 'There used to be a tennis-court.'

She's doing a water-colour study of the pool in the Italian garden. This open-air business suits her. She's rather good at painting light. Unfortunately, Amy is succumbing again to her obsession with communal living. There's a new facet to it now. Laurie needs to be integrated into the community. Her concern for his well-being may not be entirely altruistic.

'On the bottom lawn at the front. Exactly the right size. I'm sure the Victorians had one there. I spotted an old net in one of the sheds. I'll tell Guy we're *all* going to play tennis this summer. I have a feeling Laurie might be rather accomplished on a tennis-court.'

'Won't you *ask* Guy? Be tactful?'

'No point with him. He'll quibble. We'll *tell* him. Firmly.'

'Anthony wants a pool and a fitness complex.'

'Anthony will have to be restrained. We must only

develop what we can *share*. Can you see Adelaide working out on parallel bars?'

The daffodils are out around the grass in front of the flowering currant and prunus. The grounds are coming alive, the house is waking up. Once the place would have buzzed with maids spring-cleaning. Now the bright light only draws attention to the shabby paint. If only the Philosopher's House could laugh again.

Guy's opened one of the library windows and is working just within. The sun slants down on him, cutting a bright path through the library gloom. Uncharacteristic of Guy to seek fresh air. Probably the smell of the antifungal treatment on his ceiling has driven him to it. I grab the opportunity to prepare the way for Amy's tennis court. Her ton-of-bricks approach isn't going to work.

'Hello Mr Loughnian? Guy,' I say, hedging my bets, offering both respect and friendliness, the conscious compliment that the young can see that the old are not totally off the planet. I overlook his unkindness to Cob.

'Hello, Charis. Don't let me keep you.'

'How are you today, Guy?'

'Bloody awful.'

'Any particular reason?'

'My life's work,' he bellows. 'Milo was an amateur fool. Under the spell of that stupid woman. I'd thought him a rational man.' Surely he's not still on about a couple of letters. I suppose he wanted Milo to be as desiccated as himself. Disappointed or not, Guy blossoms, speaks louder when he's talking about Milo. Almost part of the human race.

He needs encouragement. And I have my own agenda. 'It's a fantastic day. Don't you feel full of

148

energy? I want to run and run. *Do* something. Ride a pony. Swim. Play tennis.'

'You'll have to make do with running,' says Guy, 'we're post-equine here, and there's never been a pool. Nor will there be. Whatever that devious toad Street-Langton says.'

'I bet you played tennis. Were you really good?'

'Not especially.'

'But you played?'

'Yes. Yes. We all did in those days. People like us.' He stares out on to the grass, perhaps seeing a younger Guy, happier and smiling, before he got desiccated. 'It was different then. Labour governments hadn't taxed us out of existence. The bloody Tories hadn't stood by doing nothing.'

'We could mark out a tennis-court beyond the shrubbery. Amy's certain there used to be one there. If everyone's not too old to play.'

'I am,' said Guy. 'Too old. We don't want any more upheavals thank you. Besides I'm at a tricky point in my work. Milo placed far too much importance on Hume. A fine mind on causality, politics, scepticism even, but when it came down to ethics, Hume chickened out. Claimed goodness results from benevolence.'

'Perhaps it does.' I'm thinking of Amy.

'Avoided the whole issue by asserting morality is outside philosophy because it's not a fixed *truth*. Morality *changes*. Absolute rubbish.'

'But it does. Fornication is almost obligatory these days.' I'm embarrassed saying this, but it's something that's been on my mind since Christmas. I'm relieved Guy ignores the remark.

'Jeremy Bentham hit the nail fair and square. Utilitarianism. Never been bettered. Believed the greatest good was what brought the greatest happiness to

149

the greatest number of people. You can't argue with that. Common sense. That's what it's all about, Charis. Common sense.'

I resist pointing out the masses want short-term gain, and usually their requirements are of a base nature. Oven-ready chips today triumph over organic broccoli tomorrow. I spot checkmate. 'The greatest good, Guy. We've *all* been talking about the tennis-court.' The smallest fib. A benevolent fabrication that Milo might appreciate.

'*Tennis*-court?'

'You need therapeutic exercise, Guy. Take your mind off Milo's letters and Hume.'

'I don't take exercise. It's plebeian. Intellectuals don't go to the gym.'

'But they play tennis,' I remind him. 'Turgenev.'

'He was a bloody Russian.'

'Amy's keen. Laurie needs the exercise. Anthony would adore to have a court. Melissa would look good in the kit. Cob *might be* athletic. Grace longs to make cucumber sandwiches. I bet you had a great backhand, Guy. Jeremy Bentham would have taken our tennis-court as a perfect example of the greatest happiness for us here. A utilitarian dream.'

'Charis. There's enough on my mind.'

'*You* don't have to do anything.'

'Preserve me from blabbering women. Like dripping taps, all of you. I don't want balls over the lawn. Above all not yellow balls. Shrieks and loud laughter from behind the hedge. Hordes of invading friends taking advantage.'

'I haven't got any friends.'

'Always got an answer, haven't you? I give up. I suppose you can carve out your blasted tennis-court. But keep it all right out of my sight.'

*   *   *

'Hello there Guy.' Adelaide saunters past, wearing a banana-coloured trouser suit. The jacket is undone. Of necessity. I've just brought Guy a comforting glass of lemonade to reward his positive attitude to the tennis-court earlier in the day.

'I'm working. Goodbye.'

'I'm off to take tea with the vicar. Any messages?'

'Why should I want to communicate with a short-arsed, asinine parasite like the Winkless?'

Adelaide adds, 'A new man. Mr Winkless. Been defrocked in the past. Only just let back into the fold.'

'*Defrocked*?'

'What credentials.'

'By the way, Adelaide. There *is* one thing. I'd like your opinion on it.'

'*Yes* Guy?' Adelaide beams and thrusts herself towards him, prow first.

'Just your *opinion*. I felt our little open day was quite a success.'

'A *success*?' Adelaide swallows. We both recall how Guy cleared the house of villagers within two minutes of walking into the library.

'We need *cultured* people visiting, you see, not rural oafs and children on the gin. We need to cast our net the length and breadth of the country. Do you think the *National Trust* might be interested in us?'

'The National Trust. Oh yes, Guy. I do think they *would* be interested,' says Adelaide. 'I really do.' She poses momentarily, already in custodial role, one arm raised casually through the open window, towards the portrait of Milo Loughnian.

'Your opinion was *all* I wanted, thank you. By the way, what was the vicar defrocked for?'

'I'm happy to say it was nothing to do with choir-boys.'

Chapter Fourteen

Amy and I push the mower together. Amy has embarked on what she calls phase three. Phase one was to get the house thinking together, to have a common purpose. Events have done that for her. Guy's roof and the need to rescue the house in order to save their homes came at a convenient time.

Phase two was getting people to eat around the same table. Despite being a lousy cook, food has a spiritual resonance for Amy. She's quite right, of course. Pagan feasts and festivals still linger on in many faiths. Hindus ritually purify their food. Sikhs have a communal meal after worship in the *gurdwara*. Grace and her church have all the significance of the Last Supper. Jewish food laws are central to the faith. Offering food is a sign of hospitality, and therefore of friendship, *agape*, the non-erotic love which is spiritual. On reflection, it's difficult to understand why our Christmas gathering was so diabolic.

The third phase is about integrated activity. An advance on integrated discussion and communal eating. I think Amy visualizes a regular programme of events. Musical evenings, gardening groups, and bridge evenings after she has learned to play. The initial activity is to be tennis. Unfortunately, the involvement is nothing like as collective as Amy wants. None of the men have offered to help.

We're re-creating the tennis-court. I would point out that when the tennis-court was redone at school, as cheaply as possible, it cost ten thousand pounds. We're doing exactly the same thing for the price of a bag of grass seed, and our sweat. Amy says empires were built on slave labour.

I imagine Victorian ladies giggling with young men in boaters on this site, knocking a few balls into the shrubbery, so they could get their bustles ruffled. The shrubbery is still here, dividing the court from the formal part of the garden. The afternoon would conclude with sandwiches and jam sponge under the trees. I'm conscious of those afternoons, as if they're still here in another form, floating in parallel with us among the weigela and hypericums. I wonder whether the past is *always* with us. Whether the past is a *part* of us.

'We'll have an inaugural tennis party,' Amy decides. 'Proper invitations. Even a poster. Everyone in the house. Even the village later. Well, perhaps not.' She recalls our open day.

Her enthusiasm is difficult to share. 'It'll take for ever to get this grass up to scratch.'

As we shove the mower to and fro, aiming at random wiry tufts and hummocks, Amy sings.

'What's that?'

'Wagner, of course. Senta's song. She rescues the Dutchman from eternally roaming the seas through her love. He's redeemed from whatever it was that condemned him.'

'Do you think the love of a good woman can redeem a man, Amy?'

'Not Henry.'

The mower reveals yellow patches randomly staining the court.

'Laurie exercises Rufus down here.' Amy smiles, her strange immobile flowering, and the gleam in her eye is intense. 'Dogs do that sort of thing. I think it looks quite pretty.'

There's a rustling in the bushes and, instead of a Victorian lady, Grace emerges, turning agonized fingers, as if she's got them under a hot-air hand-dryer. She makes an unwavering line for us. 'I've been wicked.'

'You *couldn't* be wicked, Grace.' The idea's ridiculous.

'I'm wicked about Adelaide.'

'Adelaide?'

'Don't make me speak it.'

Amy says instead, 'She's an evil old trout and you know it. Anyway if you don't confide, we'll imagine the strikingly lurid.'

Grace is reluctant, but she's gone in too far to retract. 'She's taken to going to church. It's wicked of me, isn't it? To mind my sister going to church. As if I want the faith all for myself.'

'I bet she's noisy when she gets there.'

'Exactly. As you know, I prefer the church empty, rather the services. I want to be quiet. Adelaide comes with me when I visit alone, and sits down alongside. I can't hear God at all. He almost spoke to me yesterday, but Adelaide suddenly gets up and pads to the altar to dust the candlesticks. As you know, that's my work, and anyway, they didn't *need* dusting.'

'Tactless.'

'She's a *newcomer*. We have to earn the right to care for the silver, you see. It carries a higher status than polishing the floor. In the hierarchy of service.'

'I'm sure the faith will wear off soon.'

'It's nothing to do with faith. It's the vicar. And I'm worried about the biscuits.'

'Yes?'

'She found them. The ones I leave in the vestry for Mr Winkless. He's very fond of shortbread with the end dipped in chocolate. Adelaide ate half the tin. He'll think I'm grown ungenerous.'

Amy's single-minded, and next day we're on the court again, this time with a roller. The roller's sat in a shed for decades, and all the moving parts are rusty. It's remarkably heavy. We pause for breath.

In the pause we hear a giggle. It's the giggle of a woman with a man, a flirtatious giggle. It comes from Melissa Street-Langton, and I know instinctively she's not with Anthony.

I try to get Amy to start pulling the roller again, but there's no stopping her. She creeps over to the shrubbery and peers between the bushes. I'm right behind her, though I already know what we'll see.

Walking slowly down the drive, so slowly it looks as if they're extending their time together, are Melissa and Laurie. He carries some letters, presumably on his way to the post in the village. She has a basket as if she intends shopping, which is ridiculous because she only goes out in the car, and certainly never to the village.

Amy steps back and puts her foot down the hole of a small burrowing animal. 'Ouch.'

Laurie turns to see what's going on. Melissa walks forward, trying to convey him along with her.

'Anyone there?' Laurie's touchingly concerned.

'Only me,' I say coming forward, trying to save Amy.

Amy sees Laurie approaching her and, with a flurry of gratitude, pulls her foot free and goes towards him beaming. I mean beaming. Not her usual slight jerk of the lips.

Unfortunately, her usually bloodless skin is patchily

155

red from exertions with the roller. A smear of earth from a carelessly swept hand streaks her left cheek, her hair's wilder than ever. She's not her best in jeans. Statuesque women rarely are.

Melissa comes up cool and fragrant in a floaty dress and a straw hat with a flattering turned-up brim. Hands so smooth there's clearly never been soil under *her* fingernails. Skin glows pale bronze, though there's been only a few days' sun. She *must* have been under a lamp.

'Perhaps I should help,' says Laurie. Reluctance is apparent.

'We're having a conversation,' Melissa reminds him.

'What about?' Amy asks.

'The press-cutting agency,' says Melissa.

'So what's this press-cutting thing then?' Amy leans forward, her eyes becoming a deepening grey. Serious. Interested.

'For busy important people with no time to read the papers. Want to know what's written about them. I have a list of clients. I literally cut out all the relevant bits. Nothing really.'

'It could be quite exciting.'

'It's not.'

'You read everything.'

'I have to.' There's a glimmer of humour in those strange eyes now. I wonder if he thinks Amy's mad.

'You discover about *people*. That's exciting.'

'Most people are pretty dull.'

'Observation. That's what painting's about.'

Laurie's impressed. 'Painting?'

Suddenly Amy realizes how she looks. 'We're doing the tennis-court,' she mutters. 'Think we'd better get on.' She dives back into the shrubbery, and I just catch Melissa Street-Langton with her mouth slightly parted, her eyebrows raised questioningly at Laurie. Melissa has sussed Amy's intentions out.

'Right,' says Laurie, and they go down the drive, and I just hope it's not into the sunset.

Amy and I struggle on with the roller, but she stops bubbling. She's realizing how beautiful Melissa is. It makes her work harder. Most people would get tidied up, wash their face, but Amy attacks the turf harder, gouging out errant dandelions and patches of daisies, bashing the roller firmly over potential molehills, picking up worms and transporting them carefully to the safety of the surrounding thicket.

Later she brings out lemonade and we lie on the grass looking at the sky and recovering. There could have been more cordial in the drink, it's rather weak, but Amy's running out. I lie on the grass and smell the earth, sense in my veins the throb of its heart.

Two woodpigeons fly out of the shrubbery, circle and play against the sky, their underbodies catching the light. They're as pale and delicate as the doves tumbling in Marie-Antoinette's garden at Versailles. These are only woodpigeons, common prosaic birds, ugly on the ground, scavengers, but, in the air, phosphorescent and luminous. Not heavy like feral pigeons, clumsy on their legs, alley cats of the bird world, shrieking over crusts of bread in urban squares. Woodpigeons are fractionally superior, though still common. They're my sort of birds, all I deserve. In the clear pure air they're beautiful, lovely as doves, free spirits who can achieve anything. Surely they share one consciousness, swirling together in one pattern?

Suddenly, and for no reason, I'm optimistic. Despite having seen Melissa walking with Laurie, I feel hopeful. Hopeful for us all. Between the bushes, I can see the Philosopher's House. Its grey walls look golden honey in the sunlight.

Chapter Fifteen

Grace whispers, 'I laced Adelaide's omelette with garlic. Three bulbs. She took the collection at Evensong. She must have handed over the plate just as she breathed out. Poor Mr Winkless reeled against the altar and dropped the lot. We were scrabbling about on the floor of the choir like the widow looking for her mite.'

'Should do the trick,' says Cob.

'The Lord sees into each heart and judges accordingly,' says Grace. 'I'm doomed.'

Grace's pessimism is catching. Gone is the wild exhilaration I felt yesterday in the garden. We're all doomed. The Philosopher's House. Amy's aspirations of love. Cob and I, because we'll never get our grades. I'm not bright enough. Cob has too much other work to do, so little time to revise. Sometimes I go out into the garden at night and I see the light in Cob's window long after other lights are out, skimpy blue curtains tight across the window into the small hours.

Actually, the Philosopher's House is more doomed than usual. Amy and I are reading quietly around eleven at night. I'm revising incidents where Charlotte Brontë uses the weather to echo emotions, and Amy is three-quarters through the biography of Sickert I gave her for Christmas. The light begins to flicker. A couple of minutes later there's a blast outside and the light goes out totally. 'Fuse-box is in the hall,' says Amy, and we take a torch to search for it. On the landing upstairs, Adelaide shrieks, 'Sparks. Fire. The electrics are going up.' The whole house is in darkness.

Since Guy is not on speaking terms with any of the local electricians, he has to call out the electricity board to render us harmless.

'See this,' he says the following morning. 'See what I'm reduced to.' He throws a letter he's written at Amy as we go through the hall. 'Begging, that's what it is. I've gone bowl in hand to the National Trust.'

'My dear Sirs,

'It is my understanding you are continually on the lookout for interesting properties to preserve for posterity. I am the owner of such a house. It lies on the site of an old abbey and we have now restored the original herb garden from that period. The main structure is eighteenth-century with attractive Victorian extensions. The house was once the home of Milo Loughnian, the philosopher, whose work I am editing, and hope shortly to publish.

'I would like to suggest an interim investment for maintenance, but since I have no legal offspring I would sign a deed that the house should pass to you upon my death. I can add, to encourage your optimism for this project, that I am no spring chicken.

Yours faithfully,
Guy Loughnian.'

'That's a bit extreme,' says Amy.

It's the last day of my stay here. The optimism imparted by the woodpigeons is gone for ever. This evening Cob comes round to the front door. 'Want to come for a walk?' he asks. My whole inside churns over. This is what you might call my first date. I'm *going out* with a boy, even if it's a last-minute invitation, and only for a walk.

Perhaps he sees me as not quite so plain as at first. Sometimes, especially when I'm with Amy and we're laughing, and in harmony with her small world, I see myself as not quite so plain as *I* once thought. There's more shape to my face. Grace gave me a herbal shampoo and now my hair shines with weird red lights when the sun catches it. This wasn't the promised result, but it makes me different. Just a bit. I've studied the way Melissa puts on eye-shadow, even though she never got round to teaching me. I don't go to her lengths, but I know how to make my eyes more green. Mascara gives me some eyelashes at last. I try to be as generous as Grace. Smile more, like Anthony said. I'm as eclectic as a magpie.

Cob seems to know in which direction we're going. This might be where he's been before, the evening will end up in a shed, just an excuse for a biological experience. The girls at school say that's what *all* boys ever want. After all, it's one of my own ambitions. Initiation. *The Ultimate Experience.* But not with Cob. I want Cob to like me *properly*. To want it to be *me*, not just any girl. And anyway, I like *talking* to him more than anything when he's in a kind mood.

We go out of the big gates and turn along a bridle-path across fields, alongside a hedge that is white with the hint of early mayflower. There's a gap in it, exposing a couple of bars of fence, as if the hedge were trained away to give us a view. Below, the fields drop away, and we see the village with the tiny church that Grace so loves and just the few cottages, with one other, further out than the farm. 'That's where we used to live,' he says quietly. 'We lived on the edge of the

160

village, when it was still part of the estate. Before Guy sold off most of the land and houses. Poor idiot was never capable of earning his living.'

We lean on the fence and look at this English scene. Of course it's beautiful, but not the stuff with which people of our age can fill a conversation. His elbow is touching mine. My breathing isn't altogether steady.

'That place down there is really my home,' he says. 'Not Loughnian House.'

'I know what you mean.' I'm not certain I could explain about Mum. That although living with Amy in Loughnian House is the happiest thing that's ever happened to me, it's not what I think of as home either. My home is about take-aways and dodgy paraffin heaters emitting their familiar smell, with Mum and her stories. Wild hugs and high hopes. The dizzy fear that she won't be there the next day, the anxiety that she's going to look a fool, and it'll be in the papers. The constant worry that we'll get poorer and life will become unliveable, the heady relief when things remain the same, and a cheque arrives from my father. I wish I *could* tell Cob.

'Milo's house, well, the cottage, *ought* to feel like home to me now,' says Cob, 'I've been in it two years now. But it doesn't.' He's unaware his elbow is touching mine because he's squinting into the distance, concentrating, but not seeing the village.

'Tell me why not.' In this moment I feel almost a woman. Tender and caring. I recognize my role. It's something teachers never spell out in class. At last I realize all sex education is negative, it's there to *prevent* it. If only educators could see what being a girl and a boy is about, they wouldn't be afraid. Tonight Cob and I are reassuring each other we're not totally lost. That there are people like *us*, who don't feel loved. Offering the possibility of change. If they could see Cob and me at this moment, our mentors wouldn't herd us into getting ourselves experiences we don't need.

'It's where Dad was. Playing his music. He was a professional violinist. Half Italian and half Irish. His mother came from Florence, and she named him Angelo. But his heart was Irish. Wild. Sometimes played in a gig, Irish stuff. Called his violin a fiddle then. He'd make it dance. Most of the time he played the real stuff, the core of his soul. Sometimes I can't bear to think I won't hear any of it again. It never mattered he wasn't my real father. Always had time for me, always warm. Angelo *was* my real dad as far as I'm concerned.'

'I read a poem by Hardy once. It was about his boyhood. The last line was *Yet we were looking away*.'

Cob turns to me, almost grateful. 'That's just how it was. I've read it too. I never appreciated any of it enough at the time.'

I put my hand over his, and it's cold and clammy. I know I'll be able to tell Cob about Mum after all, but not at this moment. He's wrapped up only in himself, in his loss. After all, mine isn't a loss. I have Mum there. More or less. 'Tell me again what he played mostly.'

'You want me to say it was Mozart or Brahms, don't you? Well I don't know. Titles didn't matter. I never collected them. Just knew I was happy while he played. The strange thing is . . .' Cob pauses, as if he might or might not tell me. I think he isn't going to finish, when he says, 'The strange thing is, Mum never talked about her first husband. My father. Just wouldn't. I think he must be dead. All she said was she'd tell me about him when I was eighteen. I'm eighteen now and she's not here. Everyone I ask always says they don't know. I'll never know.'

'There's always official records.'

He turns now and looks at me, those pale eyes not properly seeing *me*. 'Perhaps I don't *want* to know. Angelo was enough. Dad and the music are all I want to remember.'

'What was your mother like?'

'Always cleaning. Or cooking. Or washing. She was very proud of how everything looked. She was also proud she had Loughnian blood. Used to go on about it a lot when she was depressed. Descended from the big house, was how she put it. Like Guy. But she could never quite say how. She never had any proof. Or any real idea which relatives were responsible. It was like a folk memory. The ancestors fell on hard times some-where along the way. Funny thing is, though I lived with her for another three years after Dad died, I don't remember her now as clearly as Angelo. Perhaps because she was always there, and he came and went. He was there for special times. Besides . . .'

'Besides?'

'I don't think she loved me. She never hugged me. I never felt she needed me there. Almost resented me. She must have been attractive when she was young. Big eyes. Big hair. Laughed plenty when Angelo was home. Not other times. After he died, we were never close. Felt it was all my fault. Then she was ill, not for long. When she died, Guy said I could live in the cot-tage. I don't know why he took me in. Must have been a sense of responsibility. Having genes in common. Two years ago that was, when I was sixteen. He pro-vided for me so I could stay on at school. Social services OK'd the situation. Even so, he doesn't like me.'

'Do you think the past matters?' At this moment, the past is so conspicuous.

'The past is gone. You can't bring it back. It's weak to think about it.'

163

'I don't know what to say.'

'Just say nothing. Just be here.'

We stand for ages looking out over the village. The dying sun is a soft apricot pink.

'We should be getting back.'

We walk back holding hands as far as the gates, in sexless friendship, in mutual sadness. To our left the sun is sinking in a marshmallow cloud. It's supposed to augur good weather. As we go up the drive we break free so no-one shall misconstrue the true nature of our proximity.

I lie in my room in the turret and know I'm become a woman, in a way my first period never made me, and more of a woman than I'll be when eventually I manage to lose my virginity. This evening was a baptism of compassion. It will stay a pearl upon my rosary of life, the rosary which I shall repeat to myself as I die. If there's time.

PART THREE

Chapter Sixteen

It's almost the end of the summer term when I receive a letter from my mother. Miss Eales brings it to me, looking suspiciously at the childish handwriting combined with squiggles, flourishes and a couple of blots.

'My dear sweet Charis,

How goes it with you? I think of you so often and wish we could be together. My Nick is doing ever so well you'll be pleased to hear. He's having what's called a sabbatical from electrical wiring. He wants to be a beach bum in Corfu. My agent has been an idle bugger and failed to secure anything on the piers for me this summer. I told him, you could always try Stratford, everything's so old hat there, and my speciality is putting a new slant on a part. Did I tell you the *Leicester Mercury* critic said I had to be seen to be believed? You can't do better than that.

I've never been to Corfu, so I'm taking the opportunity to see what it's like. I remember you reading *My Family and Other Animals* for GCSE English, so it should be very nice, if a bit primitive. Nick says it might be too primitive for me, and thinks he should go ahead to suss it out. I said to him that where he went I would go too. He seemed quite surprised to find such a loyal woman. It's what he needs. Anyway, I've spoken to Amy and she has very kindly invited you for the summer holidays. Well, part of them anyway. Darling, will this be all right? I know you're happy there.

Your ever loving Mama'

I read the letter twice and triumphantly throw it in the air. When I read it a third time, I'm disturbed by the subtext of Nick's concern. Surely he knows what Corfu is like. I just hope that nothing will change before the summer holidays.

Amy decides that where the tennis-court's concerned, it's safer to have a *fait accompli* than a democratic house discussion. She organizes the opening of the court without debate. 'What we lose in collective conversation,' she says, 'we gain in communal activity. Who knows, after an introductory tournament, we might spend many a blithe summer evening with our racquets.' She uses the name of the necessary equipment with careless optimism, but, I wonder, will Grace have a racquet? Will Guy have a racquet? I doubt Cob will. I only have mine with me because I've come straight from school.

'I wonder if Laurie would let me use his computer for the notice? Perhaps you could go ahead and soften him up, Charis, make it look as if we know what we're doing. I'll pop over in about ten minutes.'

'Come in,' he says. The table is spread with folders of cuttings and a bag of apples. 'Just let me finish this. A matter of the heart. Not my usual line. Amy was quite right when she said press-cuttings work could be interesting. Don't often get the chance to make a *difference*.' He nods to himself.

Laurie traces down the columns of the cuttings with a forefinger. He spots something. His job is to recognize instantly. His mind is orderly and retentive. He's excellent at dredging, at trawling what his eyes skim.

'Amy won't be long.'

'Would you say your aunt is an intense person?' He picks up the bag of apples and optimistically waves them about, wanting them to be tidy.

'Why?'

'Megan was too intense. There was rivalry in the choir. If I got a solo, she wouldn't speak for days. If Megan got a solo, she practised all day. Through meals. In bed. I'm keen to avoid an intense woman.'

'Amy's the opposite of intense. She's state-of-the-art casual.'

'She doesn't laugh much though. Megan didn't either.'

'She does when something's funny.'

'My women have never laughed much. I'm the dull one, I suppose.' The weight of the apples tears the bag open, and they run about over the table.

'What about putting them in a bowl?' I point to Amy's sunflower languishing on top of the bookshelf.

'That'll do, I suppose,' Laurie says, and reaches for it. 'Found it on the floor.'

'The apples look great in it.' I'm forcing him to see it with Amy's eyes.

'Not too bad. Better than I thought at first.' I notice that as he gathers up the folders his eyes stray towards it, warming him, attracting him.

When Amy arrives, her face momentarily glimmers to see the bowl on the table.

*   *   *

169

It takes two hours to produce the notice, most of which is spent with Amy trying to get her imported clip-art tennis-players in scale with each other.

Loughnian House Communal Initiative
Summer Activities Programme

A tennis tournament will take place on the old tennis lawn of Loughnian House on Sunday, 25 July. Please be available at two o'clock prompt. Tennis shoes and racquet allocation will take place on court.

Amy would appreciate a line-drawing machine, a little cart you can wheel on a straight path, and the lines get painted on the grass. She makes do with a paintbrush. As an artist, Amy always insists there's no such thing as a straight line in nature, and there certainly isn't one on our tennis court. Neither do the measurements approximate to the courts at Wimbledon.

'You have to make do with what you have,' she says, kneeling back on her heels and admiring the solidity of the white paint. There'll be an interesting bounce when the ball hits that line.

'Do you think we should make a draw, Charis? If so, should there be seeding? You and Cob should be the best, with youth on your side, and it would be a pity to meet before the final. Should we have a mix-in? No. Doubles will give us more group interaction.'

'We should play it by ear. Laurie or Anthony might be the best.'

'Laurie is not athletic, and Anthony will only show off. Who knows how the afternoon will turn out? I'll cut cucumber sandwiches. Grace must cook a lemon sponge.'

By ten past two on the specified afternoon nothing much has happened. Anthony and Melissa have appeared in amazingly trendy tennis gear, headbands, towelling bracelets, bananas, drinks in sport-drink bottles with tubes sticking out of the top, the lot. Laurie leans moodily against a tree in khaki shorts, watching Melissa prance about doing what she calls limbering up.

Amy consults her piece of paper and decides it would be a pity to have all the gear on show at one time. She herself is wonderfully in keeping with the ancestry of the court, wearing a Suzanne Lenglen style of dress trailing above her ankles. It disguises her bulkiness. Her tennis shoes, instead of looking like high-powered trainers, are what my mother used to call gym shoes, canvas with thin soles and only a few holes for lacing.

'What's this hare-brained scheme?' Guy lumbers up. I'm impressed. His cream cricket trousers are held up with a necktie round the waist, the sleeves of his white shirt rolled up, and a burgundy and silver cravat. Some people can wear things round their necks without them getting all screwed up under one ear. It may be a sign of class. Like how you wear a cap. I can't wear a scarf that stays in place at all, but Guy's got it off to a T. Like Amy he wears gym shoes, but unfortunately has been gardening in them previously. Under muddy conditions.

Amy is encouraging. 'You should start us off, Guy. Would you like to partner Melissa?' Amy intends to keep Melissa away from Laurie.

'Well,' says Guy, and his lack of words is a compliment. Melissa looks fetching in her short skirt and scooped-neck top that shows off her tan so adequately. Does she need all those chains round her wrist? As she settles them further back up her arm, they enable her to wave her arm about fetchingly.

'Against Cob?' Amy suggests. I haven't noticed him arrive. He's wearing a navy tracksuit, of that old-fashioned woolly material that gets covered in bobbles, and it had. He's lurking, as if not wanting to be seen, his seagull-wing eyebrows flattened into a scowl.

'With Charis?' She raises an eyebrow at me with remarkable mobility for Amy.

I fluster at the thought. 'What about Grace?'

Grace is in a cotton frock, mauve sweet peas on a cream ground, very fresh and her eyes bright as a hamster. 'I love a tennis party,' she whispers. 'We had a court at home you know. Mother had a splendid backhand. Like a whiplash. She had to confine it so as not to beat poor Daddy.'

Melissa says, 'You sound such a happy family.'

'We were,' says Grace. 'We were. It seemed like parties all the time. We were never short of young men. Such characters. Mother was gregarious. A beauty in her day. Believed in living up to all the advantages. Though Daddy, I'm sorry to say, was a bit of a spoilsport.'

'Would you like to play first, Grace?' Amy asks.

'A bit of a spoilsport,' Grace repeats, not listening.

Adelaide strides onto the court in an acid yellow shell suit whose fabric squeaks between the legs as she walks. She's going to be hot in that. What she might have on underneath I scarcely dare contemplate. 'If you're going to dither about, Grace, I'll go instead,' she says, forgetting to keep her voice low and interesting for a moment. Melissa looks spellbound by the sight. When you have her natural dress flair it must be puzzling to comprehend how Adelaide achieves her effects. Amy restrains her.

'It'll have to be you, Charis.' Amy pushes me forward, whispering, 'Melissa won't be able to hit anything standing opposite Adelaide.' Adelaide toddles off and sits under the hedge sulking, and eating a Twix.

'Lady's mantle and yarrow,' murmurs Grace. 'I wonder if it worked.'

'What's that?' Adelaide asks.

'Nothing dear. Just some little remedy I once made up for Melissa. Of course, she never asked for it. Maybe I was wrong after all.'

The knock-up, and that's a good term for it, fails to put any of us in a good light. We rarely return the ball for the opposition to hit back. Since avoiding the opponents is what you try to do in the game, it augurs well for later in the afternoon, but shows our incompetence at the time. Anyway, it scarcely counts as a warm-up because Guy says if we don't start straight away, he'll be on his knees before the end of the set.

He serves first to me, good action but soft as a cat landing. With my eyes closed I lob it towards Melissa. She's concentrating on leaping athletically from toe to toe, rather than watching the ball. Our point.

'I wasn't ready,' she says.

'Hard cheese,' says Cob. 'Love fifteen.'

When Guy serves to him, Cob takes a huge swipe at the ball, catches it on the edge and it hits the top of the net, trickling over.

'That's not fair,' says Melissa.

When this court was in its prime, the game of tennis reflected the class-structure of Victorian society, the premium it placed on polite behaviour, the virtues of courage, formality and social graces. I sense these forces now in parallel, like a template hovering over the court, trying to shape us to its pattern. This is not our house alone. This was Milo's house. This was also the home of people in between we don't know about, like the family in the pictures on the conservatory wall, and those who chose the tiles Amy put round her Aga. There lingers, trapped in the strata of air and

173

breath, the hopes and aspirations of an intervening century. Lying on this old grass, I'm aware other lives have been here, other pain and other loves. That we're only a smaller part of the one whole. How can we think that all that matters is what's happening on this afternoon, in this one tiny part of time?

Linking us all is the Philosopher's House, up beyond the shrubbery. It's alive today because we, its lifeblood, are together and laughing. How many storms has the house seen, and how many such summer days? It has stood throughout the years, its elegance unchanging. If places like Loughnian House are gone, the roots of us all will be scarred by the loss. Our ancestry will be hidden from us. The knowledge of such houses is an anchor in our lives.

Anthony's determined to play Laurie. Has he noticed Melissa spends time talking to him? An unwise move. Laurie isn't stylish, but has the level of enthusiasm men give to Sunday cricket or football on the beach. Serious as war. He may resemble a cart-horse galloping across the grass, but his shape imposes power. Seems he's got his contact lenses well screwed in.

Anthony is the only person who knows what he's doing. His back swing matches his hair, classy but controlled. He's a schemer, placing mean little shots to parts of the court recently vacated. As in life he intends to be a winner. Amy doesn't like the look on Anthony's face and sends Grace and Adelaide on to join them, sweeten the situation.

The lady partners scarcely count. Adelaide doesn't often contact the ball with her racquet. She watches it approach, firms her stance, winds up her arm like a windmill, and the ball's gone by. Grace is wonderfully elegant, swooping down low, and following through beautifully. I notice that Laurie sometimes deliberately sends her balls she can return easily, instead of using

174

her to win the point. Amy notices this, and smiles on him benignly.

Grace is as I've never before seen her. She's got well loosened up. So slim and elegant, she could be, from a distance, a young girl again. She must have been beautiful in the way girls were only in the Twenties. Flappers. Slim. Pert. Intensely feminine though trying to look flat-chested and boyish. That look's never come back. You have to be truly innocent to display such knowingness.

Grace concentrates each time she strikes the ball, then with every success squeaks and laughs. She bounces up to Anthony after a particularly successful lob, and lifts her smiling face to him for approval. Even Anthony, obsessed with victory, laughs and puts an arm round her shoulders. In 1922 a young man would have been tempted to kiss her. Instead, he says, 'Leave everything in the middle to me.'

Anthony is intent on smashing in Laurie's head. He hits every ball directly at him, twice catching him on the shoulder, the ball having avoided Laurie's window of vision altogether. Laurie grins. Anthony sets his jaw. Maybe he's the sort of person who just has to win at games, but I don't think so. If that were so, he'd be playing off Adelaide, knowing he was on to a winner each time. He doesn't do that, he hammers Laurie.

Amy says mildly as they change ends, 'Bodyline balls aren't in the spirit of this game, Anthony.' He ignores her, so Amy says, 'Six all. An honourable draw. You can't have the court for any longer, it wouldn't be fair. We're not playing for results.'

Melissa takes no notice either. She's topping up her tan in front of an hydrangea. Guy sits beside her, one leg over the other, and supporting himself on one elbow. I try to estimate if there is a significant level of admiration. Help. That would be a further complication. I think he admires Melissa for her classiness, but that's all. He's too desiccated for passion. I wonder if he was like that even when young. There's something in Guy telling him not to try too hard for anything. That everything will come to him because of who he is. Guy is just being an eighteenth-century man sitting on the grass. Not one to sweat or demand a lager. He is in courtly pose. Guy would have fitted beautifully into any age. Other than his own.

Adelaide flops down on the grass beside me, heaving for breath. She sheds her yellow shell suit, which glints dangerously in the sun as if it might spark off a fire. Underneath are a sleeveless white blouse and Bermuda shorts, less ample than would be ideal. Her pale flesh swells out round the armpits like mature Camembert trying to escape its crust. The white towelling headband pulling her hair back from the low forehead isn't at the best angle. Melissa, sitting further along, has got her headband right, but doesn't need it. Her brow is so smooth and dry, like an apricot on a tree in mid afternoon.

Grace sets off for the house. Even though she's enjoying herself she's compelled to make tea for the rest of us. She almost skips with *joie de vivre*. Happiness has banished the stiffness from her joints. I wish she'd stay as she is this afternoon, but I bet she'll do penance again for being too happy.

What made Grace change from a wonderful girl into the devout woman she is? I say to Adelaide, who's gradually returning from the near-dead, 'I can imagine what Grace was like when she was young.'

'All the boys,' pants Adelaide, 'adored her. That was the problem, of course.'

'What problem?'

'It troubled poor Daddy no end. He was a slave to the

176

Church, poor man. Calvinist. You might have called him repressed. He married Mummy when he was very young. He *was* handsome of course. Smoked a cigar. But Mummy was a party animal. Not especially pretty, but vivacious. Poor Daddy couldn't laugh with her, and he didn't like dancing. He didn't look out to people and love them. She loved everyone. Though I don't think she ever had an affair. He was jealous of her. Not of other men, but of *her*. Of her happiness.' Adelaide pauses to catch up with her breathing. She speaks quietly, and the catches in her voice heighten the sense of tension she feels at remembering. Above us the sky is quiet in the afternoon, quiet and timeless. The same sky that might have smiled down on Adelaide and Grace when young.

'You see, Daddy saw the same joy in Grace and didn't approve. One day he caught Grace in the greenhouse, kissing James Holliday. Well, it was more James kissing Grace. Such an energetic young man. But also a socialist. Poor Daddy went bananas. He subjected her to days of moral argument. Weeks of it. Made her read bits from the Bible. The ones featuring hell-fire. Mainly from St Matthew. He brainwashed her. Literally put the fear of hell into Grace. I don't think she ever fancied another boy again.'

'He didn't do that to you, though.'

'I was lucky. I was the plain one. I slipped the net. They were grateful to get me married.' Adelaide groans as the burst of activity tells on her legs. She lowers herself to lie on her back and closes her eyes. I doubt she'll be able to clamber up on her own.

What is it about a summer afternoon, where the heat brings its stillness and the trees and buildings doze undemanding under the sun, that makes me feel sad? Is it because it is only when such stillness lulls the mind towards calm that we become aware of the weight of sadness and absent joy? The pleasure and the pain of other lives are distilled here and only in the quiet does their heaviness brush against us?

'Cucumber sandwiches,' says Grace triumphantly, staggering towards us with a tray spilling over with earthbound treats. We sprawl on the grass eating sandwiches and cake, lazy under the perfect blue parasol of the sky. Everyone should have a day like this in their lives. When they *might* reach out and find perfection. The big mistake is to *ask* yourself if you're happy.

Anthony sits cross-legged and upright, supple and fit. But not as cocky as usual. Almost wistful. 'There's something about a place like this,' he says. 'It's the history thing. These people didn't need style. Just money. They simply had it.'

'You've got both, Anthony.' Grace's benevolence beams over him.

'The money brought the other,' says Anthony, straightening out his legs, looking almost glum. Because I'm staring at him, looking a bit surprised I suppose, he adds quietly to me alone, 'And bloody hard it is.'

Now that we others have all played, Amy takes the court. I'm amazed. Arty, vague, trouble-prone Amy is a natural. I should have guessed. Those statuesque hips. She's got the weight to put behind the ball. She plays singles against Laurie, everyone else now collapsed and pigging themselves over the sandwiches and Grace's lemon cake.

It gets to be six five to Amy. Laurie doesn't look clumsy now. He's beginning to feel a rhythm, enjoying the tempo when he hits it right. Amy's hair is like a wild black halo, and her dry lips are open, gulping in air. She's elated. She's happy. She wins two points in a row.

'Set point,' calls Guy, who's fetched himself a

deck-chair and is sitting on the far side of the court, alone.

It's a long rally, and it gets faster and faster. Since Amy does no more than return the ball, Laurie's finding it easy to see. He does nothing devious or clever, as if he wants to go on hitting the ball backwards and forwards with Amy for ever. Backwards and forwards with intensifying speed. I wonder if this is what sex will be like. If it's only half as exciting, it's not something to avoid. There was eating sex in the film *Tom Jones*, but this is tennis sex.

I'm so enthralled, translating the subtext of the game, I almost miss seeing the stranger emerge from the shrubbery, a man searching for someone. He walks down the garden towards us, in a dark business suit, looking totally out of place. Is he someone bad coming to spoil the day? Is it the ghost of Grace's father coming to admonish her for being happy? My mind can't fit him in anywhere.

He looks round, trying not to focus too clearly on the tennis court. Guy sees him and levers himself out of the deck-chair.

'Mr Parcival? Welcome. Guy Loughnian.'

'Ah.'

'Come with me.' Guy leads him away. I have a sense of the ominous.

The match ends with Amy and Laurie collapsing and giggling, and saying they can't do another thing. Masses of energy expended for pure athletic pleasure. A release valve. It's done Amy a power of good. Everyone claps, except Anthony.

They come off the court with their arms round each other's shoulders, admittedly a bit like brother and sister, but it's a start. Amy looks happy.

The tennis becomes more casual. People drift on and off the court without direction from Amy. We enjoy the sun on the grass, the tea, the sound of the tennis-balls, the English afternoon. 'I might bring some of my friends over one Sunday,' says Anthony. 'Swimming-pools they all have, Saunas, snooker tables, but not many have a tennis-court.'

'Visitors have to be a communal decision,' says Amy, but only half-heartedly.

Cob sits down by me. 'Not real life, this,' he says, 'everyone pretending to be posh.' He picks a piece of grass and leans over to tickle my nose with it.

'I have worked out those letters,' he says, and I understand why he tells me this now.

'Will you show me?'

'Yes.'

'What does it say?'

'You'll have to wait and see.' The way he's looking at me is a bit disturbing. In a lovely way. My stomach's lurching, and my breathing's gone uneven. I wish this moment could go on for ever, with Cob staring at me, and as if our minds are making music together.

'Have a sandwich,' calls Grace, pointing towards the plate. I'm hungry only for the food of the soul. Or perhaps not the soul at all.

Anthony has suddenly had enough. Grown bored. He starts to clear up. Grace stacks the plates on the tray. Amy collects deck-chairs.

'If you want to see the letters,' Cob whispers, 'they're at the cottage.'

'OK.' I walk with Cob over to the cottage. We walk slowly, shyly.

As we pass the door of the studio, I see them.

Melissa and Laurie stand in his doorway. Close together. He gives her an envelope, and she looks down at it, cradling it in her hands. At this very moment, Amy comes into the courtyard with two deck-chairs, on the way to the garage shed. She follows my

180

mesmerized eyes to the door of the studio and sees Melissa standing beside Laurie, looking up into his face with childlike gratitude. She stretches up and kisses him on the cheek. It may be only on the cheek, but she lingers.

Poor Amy. She droops. Then pulls herself together and goes on to put the chairs away. I have no choice. I have to go with her back to the apartment. I have to keep talking to her. I have to obliterate the image from her mind. I have to make her smile again. Poor, poor Amy. In my life, pain and disappointment are always around the corner. It's my lot to keep them at bay.

'I've got to be with Amy,' I explain to Cob.

'Suit yourself.' Cob is cold. As I walk away he mouths something rude.

They're still there. Melissa clasping that envelope to her chest, and Laurie looking stupidly pleased with himself.

As I go in the main front door, Guy comes out with the man in the suit. I linger as long as I dare in the hall, listening to them under the portico. I need to know what this is all about. I don't trust Guy.

'I have to say, Mr Loughnian, that a library with an as yet unreconstructed ceiling, two unconvincingly furnished rooms and a Victorian conservatory are really not enough for us.'

'Perhaps we could open up another room?' Guy sounds pathetic, pleading.

'I've explained. The National Trust needs some endowment when it takes on a property these days.'

'I thought you had legacies for that sort of thing.'

'Legacies are few and far between. We use them for exceptionally important buildings. With an historical association. A famous person. Human interest. Can you delve into your history? An eccentric ancestor?'

181

Guy tries to sound modest. 'I have full documentation of Milo Loughnian, the philosopher, who lived here.'

'Never heard of him.' In the silence of the hall, I swear I hear a sigh. All that Milo Loughnian stood for seems about to be extinguished.

'So your average gawper won't have heard of him either,' Guy agrees reluctantly.

I can prolong my walk across the hall no longer. Looking up I see Adelaide at the top of the stairs, listening too. Nosy cow. I go to the task of cheering up poor Amy, but she's gone to her bed with a large brandy and a packet of chocolate digestives.

Outside, the swifts dive and swoop overhead in their eternal quest for insects. This evening they're serene and calm, coasting elegantly on the air currents. Perhaps Cob will be around. I'm too shy to go to the cottage and explain why I had to chase after Amy, that Amy's been getting her hopes up over Laurie, and they're dashed. To tell him I really wanted to go inside the cottage with him. Cob does not come out tonight.

Eventually Grace tiptoes round to Guy's apartment with a bunch of aquilegias and a whole lot more greenery. I have the gift of coinciding with other people. She peeps in through the open french window, then goes into the library. Grace is so intent on making for the table with his papers on it that she doesn't see Guy at the bookshelves on the far side of the room.

'So it's you.' Guy strides over looking threatening. Oh dear. Poor Grace.

Grace starts and drops the flowers in agitation.

'Why do you interfere in this way?' Guy demands. 'Why do all these damned flowers keep appearing in the room? Play hell with my hay fever.' He looks at Grace standing before him, strewn around with flowers and greenery.

'It's only thyme, you see,' she whispers. 'To enable you to see the fairies.'

'*Fairies*?' Guy thunders. 'Do you take me for a poofter? I could sue for less.'

'Not those sort of fairies,' says Grace. 'The spiritual world.'

'Give me strength. What's that straggly stuff?'

'Angelica.'

'What's that going to make me do? Take up crochet?'

'Angelica's sometimes called the Holy Ghost plant. I hoped it might make you . . .'

'Make me what?'

'More spiritual.' Grace hangs her head.

'I can do that with a bottle of whisky.'

'Don't mock. Perhaps I don't mean spiritual. Perhaps I mean more generous.'

'*Generous*?' Guy splutters.

'Of spirit.' Grace smiles gently, face lighting up. 'Humanity's the *only* quality you lack.'

'*Humanity*?'

'I'm afraid so.'

'My god, woman. That's impossible. My generosity is endless.' He sits down heavily on a chair. Grace slips quietly away.

Adelaide breaks his reverie half an hour later. I'm with her officially this time, not merely lurking. She brings two gin and tonics, doubles, and a slimline for me. Guy's still staring, disbelieving, into space. Adelaide says, not with particular tact, 'You cocked it up with the National Trust. I heard the man. What you need is a business manager.' She pulls three chairs and a small Louis Quinze table out through the window to where the last of the sun is on the terrace.

'You can't do that. The brocade will fade.'

'Not if we're sitting on it.' Adelaide's resolute.

'I can't take any more today,' says Guy, sitting down and accepting the gin.

'Exactly,' says Adelaide, 'which is why I'm here to help you.'

'I've had enough with tennis-balls and Grace.'

'Tomorrow I plan to organize bringing most of the furniture down from storage. Cob will decorate the top floor and we'll move you up there. Then we'll create a new eighteenth-century set of kitchens in the basement. With your advice, of course.'

'I can't be doing with all that.'

'You won't be doing with anything if you don't make some effort. Belt up, Guy. Is Loughnian House to be saved? It's me to a T. My *métier*. The National Trust have yet to be persuaded. Shall I take over the correspondence with them?'

'Certainly not.'

'You could scour the county boot sales for rusty pans and wooden rolling-pins. It'll all be quite cheap. We're not looking for an ancient range, you know. Just a hearth for a stewpot and a spit for roasting. Almost anything would do. We could even give up our sitting-room to become a main bedroom, it is a very fine room. Use our bedrooms as sitting-rooms, then Grace and I could take two extra attic rooms to sleep in. If they're good enough for you, they'll do us.'

'My god. Anyway, Mr Parcival is most unhopeful. He's not interested.'

'Honestly, Guy. Grace is going to have to strew a hell of a lot more herbs before we get any sense out of you.'

Guy stares moodily into the distance.

'Life is what you make it,' says Adelaide, and lowers her eyelids, though nothing like as provocatively as she thinks.

'My life,' says Guy, 'is shit.'

Chapter Seventeen

The next day's impossibly hot, even early in the morning. I've taken to getting up early to start cool. Amy's grilling tomatoes. There's a slight triumphal light in her serene grey eyes. 'I've had a letter from Henry,' she says. 'I shall read you the full contents.'

'"Dear Amy,
    "You're the one woman I know who will not say, I told you so. I'm sure you'll be surprised to hear from me. The truth is I've been a total fool. How could I have left such a creative and warm person in exchange for tidiness and regular meals? Honestly, I was getting terribly hungry living with you, and I was never fond of all those paintings of stems in vases with which you spent so much of your time. I should have known I was throwing away more than I gained.
    "I know now, Amy, and I'm missing you all the time. More and more. Do you think we could try and get things together again? I could buy a freezer and keep some of those prepared meals from M&S in reserve. Oven chips. Things in tins to put on toast. I'm sure we could find a way round. I've always believed I was good for you. Provided a practical

support. Remember the Aga and the studio window. You didn't have to ask twice for either of those.

"I've split up from Fiona and I'm in a small flat which is not a problem to me. I eat exclusively from foil containers, and am amazed at the high quality of most.

"Could I come and see you? Please Amy. What we had was far too special to throw away. Please, please reply and at least let me explain in person.

 your dog-eared
 Henry"'

Amy reads the letter through again, and sits on the sofa to digest the undercurrents and tone, its jauntiness and covering-up, its desperation, its boredom. Eventually she files it under the sofa and doesn't look at it again for a week.

I wish Amy had a proper bathroom. I long for a shower. I crave the feeling of sharp cold water spraying down on my back, catching my shoulder, then lifting my face up to receive the artificial rain like a lover's kiss.

Anthony goes to work. He passes our conservatory on the way to the garage, wearing a light summer suit, neutral but not too pale. He drives away with the soft top down, breeze ruffling his hair in soft caress. I wonder if Melissa would mind if I asked to borrow her bathroom. I'm sure she's got a wonderful shower. I might even get a free puff of something in a bottle. I don't mention this to Amy as it seems disloyal, but there are times when a shower is a terrible temptation.

Melissa opens the door still in her dressing-gown. My mother would call that sluttish, but Melissa could never look a slut. This is a fluffy, seriously clean towelling robe. Her face has no hint of make-up anywhere, so her eyes look nowhere near as big. Her nose is quite blotchy. There's a dribble of something on her chin. Her hair is all scraped back as if she's keeping it out of the way.

In Greek mythology Melissa was queen of Corinth, and her husband, Periander, murdered her. He did not ceremonially commit her funeral clothes to the flames in the traditional way, so when Melissa reached the underworld she roamed naked. Our Melissa's a bit like that. A soul needing her clothes.

'Hi.' Tricky situation. I don't think she's finished with the bathroom herself yet.

Melissa opens the door wider, suddenly grabs her mouth, waves her hand for me to come in, but rushes back through the kitchen and up the stairs that lead off it to the next floor. Their accommodation being partly in the servants' wing leads to this unusual arrangement. I wander into the kitchen and hear the sound of retching from above. I hope she made the bathroom.

I find another of Melissa's lists on the table. Seems she likes making lists. They *are* comforting. This list goes as follows:

Milk compound.
Gran's duck at Christmas.
The lowing of cows in the milking byre.
Milk teeth and fairies.
A dress I had when I was six that smelled of
    almond blossom.
Making junket to go with blackberries.
Peter Rabbit saying soporific.
A pink and yellow pacifier.

Melissa eventually returns, looking more herself, dressed in oatmeal shorts with a loose pink silk camisole top, tucked in. She's put on her make-up. Sadly, it wouldn't be any use me getting oatmeal shorts and that expensive top because I'd need the figure and the legs and the face to go with it, if I'm ever to emulate her style.

'Could you make some tea?' Melissa says.

The kettle's foreign with blue cornflowers on it. The mugs are blue with flowers too, and have Cyrillic letters on the base. I know the Street-Langtons have been to St Petersburg, so these might be from there. Russian pottery is style, not fashion, as Anthony would be the first to point out. I'd like some Russian mugs for my college room. If I make Durham that is. Obtaining the right mugs would be a lot easier than getting myself beautiful. They would mark me out. Identify me. I'm *not* too proud to borrow someone else's style if I have to. Perhaps if I borrow enough, I'll grow my own.

'Sorry about that.' Melissa sits down at the table and pulls a mug of tea towards her. 'All this is supposed to stop at three months.'

'Three months?' She's pregnant! If Melissa's pregnant, who's the father for heaven's sake? Just how close has Melissa got to Laurie? There was no mistaking the look of love on her face in his doorway. Is this the end of Amy's dreams?

'A mother is what I'm *meant* to be,' she says. 'I feel different, Charis. I shall be my own person at last. Just a mother. Not defined by my child. Not the mother of a particular child. Not an extraordinary child. The mother of a quite ordinary baby. Who I shall comfort in the night. Who will sleep in my arms and blow bubbles. I shall be love. It's there within me. That's what I'll be. I'm so happy. Unbelievably happy.'

'You're more than three months?' I repeat her statement, casually. I have to know the time factor. Laurie didn't arrive until Easter. Though she seemed to get on well with him in the garage right from the start.

'People are unpredictable about letting on, aren't

they? For different reasons. My reason is my figure. And telling Anthony, of course. I'm five months. You'd never guess, would you?' She turns sideways so I can admire the profile of her stomach.

'Flat as a pond.' My heart soars. For Amy. For us all. This baby was conceived long before Laurie ever walked up the drive. Why did I harbour such evil thoughts?

'The only person who knows is Grace. At least, I *think* she knows. I had a slight show at six weeks and felt too foolish to go to a doctor. I was going to confide in her. Before I could say a word, she gave me some herbs. They stopped the miscarriage.'

'I understand,' I say quietly, feeling disloyal to Amy that I'm sharing secrets with Melissa, but my heart is full of comfort. Brimming over, spilling over everything. Ample. Profligate with it. Then I remember again the way she looked at Laurie yesterday.

'Come with me,' she says. 'I haven't shown anyone else. Not even Anthony.' I follow her up the stairs, admiring the elegant way she slightly swings her hips. I try to do the same, but it doesn't feel natural. We go to a small room overlooking the garden. 'This was the old nursery. We've been using it as a storeroom.'

There are several storage cases and boxes in front of the small cast-iron fireplace, still with its guard. The curtains, almost fallen apart, have fairies with top-heavy wings hovering at intervals. But, in the corner, is a brand-new child's cot, already spread with a baby quilt, and rattles hanging from the bars. Piled at the foot are six teddy bears, all different, wide-eyed and hopeful. Beside it, a pine chest, highly waxed with transfers of Beatrix Potter animals. They belong neither to Melissa's homely Gran, nor to Anthony's stylish world.

'Shouldn't Anthony know?'

'He'll be furious. I'll lose my figure. I'll be a pudding. Pregnancy isn't *style*. Anyone can do it.'

I blurt out, 'You'll be with Anthony?' What a stupid thing to say, she'll have no idea what I've been thinking.

Momentarily she stops welling over. 'What?'

'I mean, if Anthony is going to be furious?'

'The selfish sod will have to get used to it. I just hope the baby's not too much like its father, that's all.'

'Might be a *bit* like Anthony.' I'm still seeking confirmation.

'A little bit is all it better be.'

'How do you really feel? You'll be redefined.' If I'll be redefined by sleeping with a boy, I'd be totally remodelled by becoming a parent.

'I'm happy about the baby, Charis. At least I would be if I didn't have what Anthony will say hanging over me. This is the first thing since I got married I'm going to do completely on my own. A couple of minutes at the start hardly counts. Being so dynamic, Anthony's very quick about everything he does. I've known people go to the doctor for less. My body's making this baby. My boobs will feed it. Charis, I'll be a mother. I'll be a woman.'

'It's only Anthony that's a problem?'

'He thinks he owns me. He guides my life as if it's his own. Sometimes I feel it *is* his own. I'm an extension. I'm an accessory. I'm *Anthony's* wife. *His* creation. I match the suit. I have to change all the time to fit his mood.'

'That will stop?' I see she's determined.

'No. Anthony'll either be furious because a baby isn't on the itinerary, or he'll be thrilled to have another accessory. Another extension of the wonderful stylish Anthony. It'll have to be bloody perfect. Be the first kid on our street to have an IQ of two thousand.'

'He won't live on a street.'

'You know what I mean.'

'Sorry. It came out because I've always lived in streets. Not mean streets, but unfashionable ones. Where I live never gets to be called a road or an avenue, or a close.'

'Me too. I lived in a street. Worse. A street in a village. Not a *lane*. Mother saw to it I rose above my station. I did, too. She picked out Anthony when he came to stay at his uncle's in The Vicarage, which wasn't a vicarage at all but a pretentious pile of old plumbing in a field. She spent all she had togging me up for the village garden party there. We went to London to buy the gear. It was the summer of the wispy frock, clinging and simple. Simplicity costs. And it did. Big cream roses on a straw colour. I drifted about feeling bored. It worked a treat. I got him without trying.' Melissa has this faraway look on her face, hauntingly sad.

'It was more than the dress. It must have been you.'

'It was my potential. Although Anthony was fairly middle-class, there was absolutely no money. He was determined he was going to make it. I could be the right sort of wife. A trophy. He was too proud to look for a wealthy woman, because that would have made him feel inferior. He has to achieve. He'll never stop wanting to be *envied*.' Melissa stares into space and I think she's grown bored because she doesn't speak for a while. 'He'd like to own the whole of this house, you know. Be like lord of the manor.'

'Guy's wise to that.'

Eventually she says, 'I shouldn't tell you this.'

'Oh?' I wait, not liking to think I'm going to miss something interesting. At the same time I dread she's going to say something about Laurie.

'I've always been in love with someone else.'

191

'Always?' Is this a key word?

'Since I was fifteen.'

Did she know Laurie before he came to the House and that was why she was friendly with him so quickly?

'He was a farmer. Called Jez. Three years older than me. Looked after the dairy herd in those days. My mum thought he'd never have his own farm. Never be rich. But I didn't care about that. Jez was always on my mind. That's why Anthony wanted me. Because I wasn't interested. The grass my side of the fence was fantastically green to him. Then Jez got a bursary to go to college. I worked out that if he loved me he wouldn't go. He'd stay and we'd get married. But he didn't stay. He went. So eventually I married Anthony.'

'And you think about him still?' I feel the pain.

'I've never forgotten him. Laurie's been very good.'

'*Laurie*?'

'Jez did well at college and now he's manager for a large farm complex in Yorkshire. He does a lot of experimental work on wheat. Something with genes which might avoid an allergy. I've seen his name in the papers. When I found out what Laurie does I told him all about Jez. Told him the day he arrived, actually. In the garage. When Laurie said he had to read every newspaper and journal. He's been looking out for references for me. He'd found a couple of small items the day we saw you making the tennis-court. Nothing that told me anything about Jez himself.'

'I *see*.'

'Now he's found some real information at last. Gave it to me yesterday. After the tennis. Said he didn't want to upset my game by handing it over earlier. Something about a genetic breakthrough. In a scientific magazine. I was so excited when he gave it to me. Now, I wish I'd never read it. There was a potted biography at the end. It mentioned his wife. She's called Jane. I didn't know about Jane.'

I can think of nothing to say.

Eventually Melissa continues, 'Money's not what will make me happy. I want kindness. Gentleness. Jez was so warm. Always good-natured. He never worked in a tie.'

'You'll stay with Anthony?'

'I can't take his child away from him can I? And if I ever found Jez again, he's got Jane now. Two wrongs don't make a right.'

Sometimes, common sense can lead more certainly to good, than philosophy or religion. I can see Melissa's always had common sense. 'Jez sounds great.' I drop this out by way of consolation, but she'll never realize how sincerely I mean it.

Chapter Eighteen

The post-box system at Loughnian House is never easy. Inexperienced postmen often mix up the mail. If the big front door is open, they're supposed to put the occupants' post into the named trays on the marble-topped table near Amy's door. This morning, I'm looking to see if we have any post, perhaps another letter from Henry for Amy, or one from my mother. Anthony's pile always contains more than the rest of ours put together, and proper letters, not unsolicited. I'm idly wondering why a letter addressed to Guy is in Anthony and Melissa's tray.

Before I can sort this out, Anthony rushes out of his door and grabs his pile. 'Cheers, sweetie,' he calls to me over his shoulder as he speeds out of the front door. 'You and Melissa going to knock a few balls about later?' I think he's working on stopping Melissa from getting bored with the country. He doesn't wait for a reply. I fail to point out he's got one of Guy's letters. I wonder if it's important. I think it had a bank emblem in the corner. It didn't look like the rest of Guy's unsolicited envelopes.

Next morning, I see the letter again in Guy's tray. The flap is no longer neatly stuck down, the paper is buckled and wavy. Tentatively, I pull at the corner, and it comes away from the rest of the envelope quite easily. Anthony must have steamed it open. Since it's virtually open anyway, I see no reason not to check up on what Anthony has discovered about Guy and the bank. If only for Guy's sake.

My dear Guy,

Usually it's all computerized letters these days, but since I've known you for so many years, and recognize you as an honourable gentleman I thought we'd do better here with a note in my hand. The problem lies in the surfeit of figures in the left-hand column, a deficiency of numbers in the centre, each to the detriment of the balance on the right. I think it would be helpful to both of us if we were to have a little chat. Could you make an appointment and drop in during the week?

Certain we won't have a problem,
Maurice.

Oily creep. I only just get the letter back in the tray when Guy himself comes out of his apartment.

He picks up the rest of his post, reading this letter on his way across the hall. He mutters to no-one in particular, 'Loathsome cretin. Dropped off the bottom of somebody's boot.'

'Come with me, Charis,' Adelaide calls through the conservatory window. 'I may need you to take minutes.'

Adelaide is set up in managerial role, something she's been working on ever since the National Trust dumped Guy. She's unmissable in a vermilion suit, of which the skirt is too short, so she's constantly bending her knees, hoping they'll disappear under the hem. She clasps a clipboard under one arm, and three coloured pens project challengingly from her top pocket. This is not the Adelaide who embroidered the history of the Philosopher's House on Easter Sunday. Adelaide has passed beyond the genteel role of National Trust guide. She has become business manager and dowager simultaneously. If she knew the first thing about computers, we'd have our own web site before evening.

We sail unstoppably through the open french doors of the library. 'If you're not part of the answer, you're part of the problem,' she booms at Guy.

Guy is standing beside his open safe, which is usually hidden behind the botany books section. He's staring at an oblong, yellowing paper, so thin I can see there are specific sections and areas for information. When he sees us, he stuffs it back into the safe, presses a button to make the safe disappear. The only document I can think of being the same shape and design is my birth certificate.

Surprisingly, Guy does not resist. 'See what's come now.' Guy points to his desk. Adelaide reads the letter out loud.

'"Dear Mr Loughnian,

"You may not immediately recognize the name of my company, but I would of course be happy to supply you with whatever information necessary to satistfy any queries you might have about our past successful transactions.

"To be brief, in my first letter to you, Mr Loughnian, my interest is in bringing affluent attractive families together with expensive, exquisite properties. There are many successful people today who are capable of maintaining our heritage in the way that it should, while at the same time there are esteemed genteel families who lack offspring to inherit, and worry about the future wellbeing of their much-loved home of many centuries.

196

"I have heard from a source, Mr Loughnian, from a gentleman who is aware of all the great homes in the Midlands area, that you may have such a concern. I write, wondering therefore if we can be of any service to you. I do have on my records at least three families who might favour your area, and who are people of taste and perception.

"I assure you, Mr Loughnian, sensitivity is our byword. Integrity is our watchword. If you feel we could be of any help, please get in touch.

      Yours sincerely

      James Wright."'

'How dare a little worm called James Wright presume to write to me, unsolicited. I hate people who keep repeating your name. And who the bleeding heck are these people of *taste and perception*?'

'Do you see this as your last throw, Guy?'

'It will be if Maurice sticks with his gutter principles. He's the sodding bank manager.'

'They may not be people of taste and perception. They may be property developers.'

Guy's jaw drops below its usual miserable level. 'I'd rather the house fell down over me than be some filthy modern estate of twelve tasteful dwellings with self-maintaining window-frames.'

'Then we've got to go for it.' Adelaide is hoarse with determination. 'You were turned down by the National Trust because you didn't offer enough. We've got to get together what professionally I call an *attractive business package*.'

'James Wright sounds less trouble.' Guy is pathetic. Struggling. Like a wasp that's been swatted not quite enough.

'Why don't you show that letter to Laurie?' There's something about it makes me suspicious. I'm not sure where this suspicion comes from, but I feel uneasy; it isn't what it seems. Perhaps because I know Anthony opened Guy's letter from the bank, and I remember how I saw him, from my bedroom window, size up the back of the house.

'What for?'

'He might trace something.'

'Trace what?'

'Don't you think the letter's a bit odd? Do people really do what he claims?'

'Worth trying,' says Adelaide. 'Sounds fishy to me, as well. You'll make me a useful PA yet, Charis. And in the meantime, Guy, I believe we should make a fresh approach. You must do exactly as I say.'

Melissa's in two minds about Guy's proposal. She ticks over. 'I don't fancy strangers in the house.'

'One day a week, and only the dining-room,' says Adelaide briskly. 'But you get to use the furniture for the other six. You'll have much classier dinner parties.'

Melissa contemplates the present furniture, the finest individually designed that Anthony could locate. Brass-banded cherry corners, and satinwood inlay in the sideboard doors.

'Anthony's a man to appreciate antiques.' Guy's being oily.

'Do any of your friends have dining furniture with four noughts on,' Adelaide asks, 'not counting the pence?'

Melissa knows Anthony will succumb to noughts. Style itself may exceed noughts, but noughts are the foundation of style. Might even put him in the mood to hear about the baby. 'Well,' she says, doubtfully.

'Consider it done.' Adelaide is brisk. 'Anthony will not regret it.'

'Anyway, we eat in the kitchen,' says Melissa, 'or we go out.'

We have accumulated a further room to impress the National Trust.

'Next,' says Adelaide, and marches out.

It's a pantomime to get the furniture back downstairs from its upstairs storage, dining-table, chairs, also buffet sideboard, wine coolers and coasters. Guy fetches Laurie to help Cob and himself. Adelaide supervises. Amy makes helpful suggestions. Just as the sideboard threatens to slide down and crush Guy's fingers, Amy comes out with, 'Henry wants me to go back to him.'

'What's that?' Laurie asks, and lets go of his corner.

Guy leaps up, and misses the sideboard as it slides down the last of the stairs, out of control. He asks, 'Does that mean your apartment will be vacant?'

Amy, oblivious of any danger to Guy, says, 'I'm still considering what to do about my husband.' Then she goes off to do some more *plein air*. The gallery's asking for white marguerites. Amy's giving them acanthus because she's in a blue period. I saw she'd stocked up on yellows last week, ochre, primrose, chrome. *Eventually* she'll be into marguerites, except the gallery will have gone off them by then. That's Amy for you. Never quite where the action is.

Cob and I polish the table again. It's picked up a grey bloom since Christmas. Sometimes we move together and our elbows accidentally touch.

'You look like Charlotte Brontë.'

'Oh. The paintings of her. She was awful.'

'Probably Bramwell wasn't much good as an artist.'

'I'm thinking of the drawing by George Richmond. The one on my cover.'

'She's OK.'

199

'She's plain. You can hardly see her eyelashes. Her bones are splodge. She's got a long nose.'

'So have you.' Cob doesn't look up. 'Got a long nose.'

'I know.' I want to cry. I despair for poor Charlotte Brontë. Unlucky in love, and in death too. I despair for me.

Cob says, 'I like girls with long noses.'

'You do?' That's wonderful. I thought big noses cancelled out green eyes. Now I see they're complementary.

'I think,' says Cob, 'I'd only tell a girl with a big nose what's in Milo's letters.'

'I'd forgotten about those. With the A level results looming.' I can lie as well as anyone. I'm not letting on I keep thinking all the time about how I didn't go to the cottage to see them.

'There are three letters as well as the two I gave to Guy. I shall show them to him at the right moment.' He throws his duster on the floor. 'Think that's as good a shine as we'll get.'   .

Cob fetches the letters, not suggesting we go to the cottage this time. Perhaps he fears rejection more than I do. Before he comes back, Anthony strides into the room, all energy and dynamism, to inspect the table. He examines it from all angles. Then he stands beside me and casually slings an arm around my shoulders. When Anthony's pleased with something he likes to distribute the pleasure of his physical presence to others.

'You know, Charis, I believe I've learned something new today. Having style doesn't *have* to be leading the pack from the front. Being ahead all the time. There's a hell of a lot of style in our aristocratic past. Don't you think? I like it. I like it.' His arm drops from my shoulders and he speeds out of the room to pursue his next project, knocking into Cob returning.

'Pleased with his new acquisitions, is he?' Cob puts the letters on the table, eyebrows an impish arch, mouth a lopsided smirk. 'Now you can discover who Milo knew.'

'Who?'

'Would you like me to read them out to you?'

'"The eleventh day of March 1759

"My dear Milo,

"I much enjoyed my brief sojourn with you, and felt the hospitality of your house and your table and cellar to have provided great physical happiness to my old bones. I am profoundly apologetic for the misfortune to your chair.

"I much enjoyed the double aspects from my bedroom windows both to the South and to the East of your fine Hertfordshire countryside. More mellow, I freely admit, than my beloved Scotland. Also, it was extremely kind that you should allow me use of your library for the whole day in which to work on my third volume of *The Histories*. Tranquil, the hours spent there.

"I feel a great and overwhelming sympathy for your predicament, as regards Lady Elizabeth Fraser. And the sorry tale of her injured husband. It is, as you say, fairly obvious rightful behaviour not to cause pain to the others concerned, should you successfully follow your inclination. My concern now is for you. For the anguish with which you wrestle.

"Your decision is one of cold rationality, and as you full well know I have never believed that to arrive at a concept of good through reason is a satisfactory path to tread. I am justified in this belief now when, and I apologize for thinking thus, I see your torment. Right behaviour as the result of feeling would bring you to a happier stance, I do believe. Quite the opposite approach than my calling of philosophical thought would seem to suggest.

"My dear fellow, I know your first feeling would be of emotion for the lady, and you at this point will imagine that I'm advocating a quite different path of pursuit. Quite otherwise, I assure you. The supreme moral good is benevolence. It is an unselfish regard for individuals and for society where there exists no reason for you to think thus.

"Generosity. Yes. Generosity from the heart. Benevolence, if you prefer. It spills over into life and illuminates the hidden places of the spirit (for which there is no possible evidence) but it is a word I can feel free to use when we venture into the unphilo-sophical world of feeling.

"Do you not see, my dear fellow, that if you arrive at your decision through your heart, you will experience not sorrow, but exhilaration and joy? You will recall that Socrates also believed that good, though in his belief arrived at by rational thought, leads to feelings of happiness and so would be accepted as the right path. A different approach; the same conclusion. What nonsense our philosophy is.

"I hope to hear from you at a later date and that you are much recovered in spirits and back to your usual enquiring frame of mind.

Your loyal friend
David Hume."'

'David Hume?' I look at Cob. 'The David Hume *we* know about? The philosopher?'
'Yep.'
'How do you know that?'
'Just listen to the next letter. It's from Milo to Hume.

I think it must be a copy. I don't see he would have had the original.'

         '"First day of April 1759

"My dear David,

    "How I wish you were still in London overseeing the printing of your two new volumes. But you are hundreds of miles away in cold and distant Edinburgh. How much I enjoyed your company at my house when the journey from London to Hertfordshire was so much less of a toil.

    "How great was the privilege of your actual presence, even more than living in your written word. How can I even begin to say that even more precious than your corporeal presence was the company of your mind in our discussions, which we pursued so late into the small hours. It was a joy to me that considerably lightened my heavy heart, the reason for which I confided to you, and which you so concernedly gave your sympathy.

    "I have to thank you for your great understanding in the matter of the lady who resides in my heart. I confess to a little too much of the claret, though how one can have anything too much of so fine a bottle, I know not. I fear that might have been responsible for your unfortunate tumble from the dining-chair. I shall never forget the moment, my dear David, for once we had established there was no injury to yourself, it did indeed have a humorous slant. You gave such a roar, such as befits your fine frame, and you burst forth from the chair in a most exuberant manner. It had always been a well-made chair, but I fear it will never be quite so secure again.

    "To matters of greater importance. I have before me the two volumes themselves of your *History of England*. Hot from the press. Before they are available to your adoring public. I feel so privileged to hold them. They arrived by coach this very morning, direct from London. I shall take much pleasure in reading slowly and carefully your account of the Tudor forgers of our island chronicle.

With my constant affection

Milo Loughnian."

'The *History of England*, you see. He wrote four volumes. It proves it is him.'

'And that must be how the chair got broken. Guy will be chuffed to know David Hume broke his chair.'

'*When* he knows,' says Cob.

'You said there were three letters.'

'This last one's not so good. It's written to Elizabeth, but he never sent it. Wrote it, and kept it himself. As if he had to write it, because it seemed like he was speaking to her. There was no point in sending it. There's no date. She died in childbirth.

"My dearest Elizabeth,

"Only last week did I receive the news you have died. I have to accept that Elizabeth Fraser is no more. I cannot believe that you are not still in the world, my world, illuminating it even when you are out of sight. That you died giving a new life is all the more bitter, for there are still these old lives that have so much greater need of you. I have spent days of disbelief, but now I can hold the truth, face it in my mind, within myself, face that which I could never have considered possible.

"I come to none of these decisions through the reason I have trusted for so long. Reason is not alive. It does not burn. I have kept away from you because I could not bear to see you tending your husband with the tenderness I know is within you. I wanted to protect myself even more than I desired to see you. Perhaps if I had listened to that dear man, David, more closely, I might have lived a different life altogether. I might have felt a benevolence to all, a non-erotic love that might even have included you. It is the heart that lives, Elizabeth, the heart that should be our guide. Generosity. For had I been a fellow of greater benevolence, I could well have been your friend, even if not your lover. There might have been room in your life to acknowledge me. But I have been cold. Rational. Too fond of reasoning.

"I have more pain to bear than those who were with you, I believe. You have gone from all our lives, and from a greater part of others closer to you than from mine. But, you see, they did have you within their lives, and I only had you for so few hours. Moreover, though I am reluctant to admit this to myself, I know from the tone of your letter I was never more than an amusement to you, a game to while away the time your husband was away in the war. Your husband has this new child. Your other children have a thousand memories. Your friends have known your laughter over many hours.

"You were nothing that was mine. Although I hoped otherwise, you probably carried no thought of me, no memory colours your departed soul. You are not mine to mourn. I have no love of my own. Not one word of love has passed between us since that one night. Only so few words then.

"I have lost you, my love, but most sad of all, you have never been mine to lose.

"I intend to do a wicked act. One that may be discovered or not. I cannot live in this world when you are no longer here, Elizabeth. I have the necessary laudanum.

"I shall hide these outpourings of my heart. Shall

hide them from the prying eyes of neighbours and cousins, who will arrive when I am gone. They shall know nothing of what has been immaculate to me. Why don't I destroy these letters and keep my feelings safe for ever? In asking this question, at least I am honest with myself until the last. I hope I am honest. It is because if the writing remains, and should there be no more to life than our sojourn here, then my love will not be entirely extinguished. It will not disappear totally from this earth. It will exist hidden in these letters.

"Farewell, Elizabeth. I shall be gone within the hour. I shall secure the papers within the library, and return to my room alone. I am uncertain how long before the medicine will claim me. It is a full four hours until supper, and I shall not be disturbed."

'I guessed,' says Cob. 'Remember the graveyard? The only way Milo's grave could be immediately within the wall after the area was extended was if he was originally buried outside. In unconsecrated ground. I guessed then he'd committed suicide.'

Chapter Nineteen

'Come for a walk,' says Cob. He comes into the conservatory from the garden. Amy is out seeing Grace. He looks well scrubbed, his hair wet and brushed back. It's quite late and the swifts are flying low in the pale evening sky.

'Not long now,' says Cob, as we go towards the drive. 'The results. One more day.'

'I'm scared.'

'Me too.'

We walk down to the gates and turn left away from the village. We go on for ever into the fields and walk until it gets dark. In the distance I can see the cottage where he used to live, but this no longer seems to bother him. He doesn't glance in that direction at all. For the first time we talk easily, about all sorts of things, personal things. How I feel about my family, what he can remember of his.

'Do you ever feel Guy is family?'

'Not properly. It's so distant. And I don't feel this place is home either. Do you know what I'd really like? To live in a house that's nearly all glass. So I don't feel closed in. And I'd like it to be round, something without corners. Things get stuck in corners.'

'Like dust. Like the past. Have you given Guy those last three letters yet?'

'No.'

'Would cheer him up. He's so sad about Milo. As if the pain was his own.' The field path runs out, and without saying anything we turn back, retracing our steps.

'I suppose keeping them gives me power. Knowing something Guy doesn't know.'

'They belong to Guy, if they belong to anyone.' I take hold of his hands and make him look me in the face. We stand there for ages looking at each other. Part of me is singing. The rest of me is still the stupid, gauche, useless idiot I've always been, afraid, unsure, untrusting.

When he kisses me, it's not magic at all. Just rather wet.

At the gate Grace is coming the other way. She's been to church. Again. She's been crying, and tries to hurry up the drive before we reach her.

'What's the matter?' Cob is gentle, caring. Why does he have to be so cocky most of the time?

Grace sobs, 'I don't like her doing it. It's not dignified.'

'Adelaide? She's not still after Mr Winkless, is she?'

Grace plays with the hem of her cardigan, looks up appealingly at Cob. 'She chases after Guy. Acts like she's the lady of the house. It's not right.'

I remember the penance on the stairs. Of course. Grace is in love with Guy. She always *has* been, ever since she and Adelaide moved into that apartment, years ago. Poor Grace. Seeking comfort for it in religion.

The world divides between those who welcome the cold truth, and those who need the warmth of certain faith. Call it blind optimism. Call it the hope of ultimate perfection. Faith, or its absence, does more to inform a life than money or laws or instruction.

Even David Hume, who *was* a philosopher, realized reason can't be the ultimate navigator. He looked to generosity of the heart. He looked within.

Grace looks to her religion, but if Jesus had never lived, Grace would be as good, Grace would be unendingly kind. She has her own secret fountain of benevolence. Guy, whose heart must be as shrivelled as his face, only behaves like a gentleman because he thinks it out, or because someone told him what to do in the past. Amy has a generous spirit. Adelaide and Anthony do not. Mum? Well, Mum *would* have a generous heart too, if she were not so constantly taken up with her love life.

What of me? It's as if I live in a wood, and only sometimes does generosity come to me, like a fitful sun percolating through the trees. I must get out of the wood and try to feel the compassion of the earth more clearly. I haven't found my path yet, but at least now I know it's there.

'You're the kindest, most caring person I've ever met, Grace.' I want to tell her she has enough strength within herself, that each way must be one's own.

'The gift of the Lord, Charis dear.'

Cob sounds angry. You've got to get on top of religion. It's choking you. Religion tells you what to do. Takes away the responsibility of thinking for yourself. It stops your heart talking. *Listen* to yourself, Grace. You know better than most people.'

Cob stomps back to the house, as if he's forgotten me. Honestly. I could hit Grace for turning up at this particular moment.

'Oh,' says Grace. 'What a passionate young man.'

*   *   *

'Can I come in?' Laurie is at the door with an envelope.

Amy nods vaguely, absorbed in her work, and gestures him in with a quick flick of the wrist. I wish she'd spent more time brushing her hair this morning. It's wild to the point of being weird.

'You said my work could be interesting,' he says tentatively. 'Learn about people. That's what you said.'

'Right,' says Amy. 'What do you think?' This time only a finger flicks out towards the yellow day lilies.

'Lovely,' says Laurie, and tries to get back on track with his conversation by holding up the envelope. Amy grunts and turns back to the canvas.

'Well, I've learned something very interesting,' says Laurie. 'I've brought you this.' He hands Amy the envelope with what is almost a little bow. It's how he would hand over roses. I'm momentarily optimistic.

'What is it?' Amy obviously is not struck by the sub-text of the gesture. If she were into body language at all she wouldn't be so restrictive with her own.

'It's information for Guy really. I wanted you to know I'd done it. I've already given him a copy.'

'Oh, leave it on the table.' She flicks her brush briefly across the canvas, lifting the tone, a subtle change in the shadows.

'Have you thought . . . I mean . . . what's . . . you know, your husband?'

'I'm still considering Henry's offer,' says Amy unhelpfully. 'There's a lot going for Henry. But then, there's plenty against. The jury is still out.'

Laurie says, 'I see.' He walks away, rejected.

I watch Laurie kick at a stone on the path. 'I think it's you he likes, Amy.'

'Rubbish. Never shown a spark. Just once playing tennis. Then he was cuddling up next minute with Melissa. He's not interested in me.'

210

'I explained to you about that incident. It was to do with Melissa's Jez.'

'Maybe.'

'You could have paid more attention to what he brought you, Amy.'

'What's the use? Did I tell you I had another letter from Henry? He still wants to come back. I thought he'd only written the first time in a low moment.'

'He's a weasel.'

'He was my husband. I liked being married to him.'

'You said you were over him.'

'I am. But I liked being married. It's comforting to find someone else's feet in bed with you.'

It's Thursday. The results are due.

The postman usually comes around ten. Cob and I intercept him on the drive. I don't open my envelope until Cob has torn at his. I wish this moment would go away. I wish it were over. 'What have you got?' My voice is dry.

'An A. And two Bs. I can't believe it. Masses more than I need.' His hand is shaking. 'Get on with it, you.'

Slowly, and feeling sick, I tear at the envelope. 'Three As. God. I've done it.' And promptly start crying. Quite hysterically. Laughing at the same time. Cob's got tears all over his face too. Neither of us can speak.

Cob hugs me, and we cling together, not as boy and girl, but as two persons who thought they were going to drown, and now cling safely to a raft. Our lives are saved.

There's a second letter for me. It's from my mother, and her tears have smudged the ink. Nick, her young electrician, has bought her a ticket to return home, and she'll arrive late on Friday. She caught him with the girl from the bar. A little tart, all Greek eyes and floppy boobs. About twenty. Mum lurches between maudlin misery and spirited wrath.

'I'll have to go home tomorrow,' I tell Cob.

'We'll celebrate,' cries Amy, taking our hands. 'I'll cook us a wonderful meal. We'll ask everyone.' She stands before the Aga, expecting inspiration.

At six o'clock, Adelaide takes two gin and limes round to Guy. Their culinary economies have given Adelaide the impression she can afford to drink spirits. They sit outside the library, at a wicker garden table. Because I'm conveniently passing, I'm invited to join them.

'This is very civilized,' says Guy. 'Very nice indeed.'

'A good habit,' says Adelaide.

'Quite reminds me of Greece,' says Guy. 'I went to a lecture tour in Athens once, you know. Not too bad for abroad.'

'*I* like Greece,' gurgles Adelaide. 'I know an excellent beach in Cyprus. Mini-bar and a waiter will bring out your lunch. Fancy us having Greece in common.'

I doubt Guy's listening to her. He continues, 'I'm rereading *Essays Moral Political and Literary* by David Hume and edited by Eugene E. Miller. Quite excellent.'

Adelaide giggles. 'Another coincidence. What I'm reading must be by his brother, Henry. The tropic of something. That's excellent as well.' Adelaide slakes her lust on cheese sablés and cashew nuts. She's decanted the packets into ramekin dishes, instead of pigging out of the bag as she usually does.

'Cultural conversation, of travel and of literature. This is really very pleasant, Adelaide. So good of you to take some of the housekeeping irritations out of my life.' Guy smiles. Not a sour and reluctant reshuffling of the features, but with a glimmer of pleasure.

*   *   *

Amy tells everyone seven o'clock, but, of course, we're nowhere near ready by that time. She finally decided on chicken casserole with strange and meaningful additions. Raisins for fruitfulness. Pineapple for colour in our lives, apricots for sweetness. For reasons known only unto Amy, she decides to serve this with what she calls onion marmalade that she makes on top of the Aga. Amy's forgotten that if you do too much cooking on the plates, the ovens cool off. At seven o'clock the fork won't penetrate the meat. Fortunately, she stipulated *bring a bottle*. The *bottles* comprise elderflower chardonnay in a lemonade bottle, a litre of whisky, red wine of unknown source with a £1.99 price ticket, a pack of Fosters, some cider and a half-crate of Mersault. We could have a game, guessing who brought what.

We languish about in the sitting-room, cheek by jowl with a basket of ironing, an easel, two wet canvases and a couple of coffee-mugs left over from lunch. Laurie has some new specs. Not only do they lend *gravitas*, they should stop that interminable fishing about on the floor after his lenses.

'How are your problems, Guy?' Anthony is casual. 'The roof and all that. Coping, are you?'

'There's the possibility of a solution.' Oddly, Guy's eyes light up as he says this.

'Yes?' Anthony couldn't be more offhand.

'An offer from some frightfully ingenious fellow. James Wright, if I remember correctly.'

'Going to accept, are you?'

There's a pause. A long pause. Guy looks Anthony fully in the eyes. 'Not quite made up my mind.'

Because I live so much of other people's lives I see Guy's playing a game with Anthony.

Laurie says, 'Didn't you read my notes, Guy?'

213

'What notes were those?'

'I gave you an envelope.'

'So you did. I suppose I must have lost it among my papers. Most careless of me, Laurie.'

'I traced who James Wright is. He's a property developer. Calls himself Village Life Homes. He buys up prime rural sites, then builds economy houses cheek by jowl. Jerry-building. Most village properties are expensive, out of reach. He's got a ready market.'

'Oh.' Guy slumps. 'Well, it might still come to that.'

'I've already made my position clear,' says Anthony.

'Not exactly a solution if we're all out on the street,' snarls Guy.

'But you'd have the cash.' Anthony shrugs. He finds it hard to understand that money is not on the top rung in Guy's priorities.

Cob is staring at Guy. Then looks at me and smiles. What a smile. The knife-edges and arrow angles of his face soften. For a moment there's the touch of an angel about him. Or maybe he's thinking of David Hume's benevolence. 'There's something you ought to see, Guy.'

'You deceitful little parasite. What are you playing at now?'

'I knew there'd be a right moment.' Cob pulls an envelope out of his shirt pocket. The envelope is new, and inside are the three letters, two written by Milo, one by David Hume. Looks like he meant to hand them over this evening all along. Anthony, the sale no longer a topic, wanders off to the bottles.

Guy takes time to digest the first two letters. He keeps looking from one to the other as if he can't believe what he sees. Eventually he beams round at us both. 'This is wonderful stuff. David Hume broke the dining-chair. We have provenance. Proper proof. Not hearsay. That's what history's made of. Not wars, not Parliament or kings. Ordinary life. David Hume has been in this house and broken my dining-chair. Britain's finest philosopher. The man who turned philosophy on its head.'

'You said he was rubbish. A useless atheist, you said. You approve of him now, do you?'

'If he's been in this house, I certainly do.'

'Do you realize,' asks Guy, 'that Milo Loughnian sat in *my* library and read one of the first copies of Hume's great histories?'

'*His* library,' Cob points out.

Guy ignores him. 'What is especially interesting is that what Hume writes to Milo is exactly what he says in his *Essays Moral and Political*. Something to the effect, *morality is not the conclusion of reason*. He argued that reason should lead to truth, but that morality is not a truth because it varies within the passage of time. Expressed here in his own words to a friend. To Milo. This letter's worth something, you know. But it's not for sale. It's worth more to the Philosopher's House.' Guy reads the signature again. His breath flutters and he momentarily lays down the paper.

'I've always suspected it. Not so much *thought* it, you know. *Felt* it in my bones. That great men have been within this house.'

Cob nods.

'David Hume's *worked* in *this* house,' muses Guy. 'A wonderful concept for me. Even better for the future. You know, I think the time has come to move forward.'

'Yes?'

'Adelaide has plans. I didn't think they were enough. But now we have a *character*. The chap from the National Trust spoke of the importance of association. We've got that now. We could work out which bedroom David Hume slept in. Bloody hell. It's

215

Adelaide's sitting-room. Need to find a four-poster. Some nicely faded tapestry. Washstand. A wig stand, do you think?'

Cob says, 'Perhaps you should read the last letter, Guy.'

Chapter Twenty

'Another twenty minutes,' calls Amy. The salad's beginning to wilt. She sprinkles the leaves with water.

Anthony says, 'Come on chaps. Drink up. We're celebrating exams.' Only Melissa sticks with orange juice. She looks nervous. In a loose shirt, embroidered with white roses, she's not her usual svelte self. It must be getting near confession to Anthony time.

Anthony inspects the conservatory. Adelaide has brought over a card-table, and Guy's provided extra chairs, but it's cramped. 'Why don't you guys all come over to our dining-room?' Anthony suggests. 'Sit in comfort round Guy's table. In a bit of style.'

Amy hesitates, after all she has arranged all of this. However, still eager to encourage every gesture of togetherness from others in the House, she says, 'So long as we come back here for coffee.'

We eventually sit down to supper forty-five minutes after our stomachs are ready. The windows are open on to the evening air which smells of cut grass. Cob was out with the mower after tea. Anthony has invested in heavy silver cutlery to go with the table. Gone is the slender Swedish stainless steel used at Christmas. There is also now a chandelier suspended above our heads.

Being more sober than we were at Christmas, we get the casserole to the dining-room without incident. Once the food is on plates, Amy relaxes. For Amy, the chicken's not bad, only tough in small areas. Anthony sits at the head of the table, with an air of supremacy, as if he has every right to be the head of this gathering. Authority sits easily upon him.

Guy glowers. He says, 'Do you have a telephone here, Anthony. I need to make a quick call. Need to do a deal. Sort of thing you do all the time on your blasted mobile.'

Anthony looks older tonight. His gloss is smudged. Mouth clenched more obviously than usual. Anthony won't age well. He hands Guy his mobile knowing he won't manage to make it work. Guy's never used one in his life, and makes a mess of the dialling. Anthony shows him how, but Guy still has to do it twice.

'Just getting on to the National Trust,' he tells us as he waits for a reply. 'I know a fellow there who deals with this sort of thing. Thoroughly decent chap.' Guy holds up a finger to show the ringing has stopped. His expression is almost impish.

'Mr Parcival? Sorry to trouble you on your home number. Guy Loughnian here. Loughnian House. You remember? Yes. You were a little doubtful when we met earlier. However, discoveries are made. Visits have come to light. Would it make a difference that David Hume once stayed in this house? I take it you *have* heard of David Hume? That he *dined* here? That we have the chair in which he sat, and proof that he *broke* it? We know the bedroom in which he slept. That he *worked* on the later books of his *History* here?'

Guy gazes at the ceiling, listening to the response on the other end of the line.

'Yes. Yes. Of course I mean the philosopher, David Hume. We have the correspondence to prove that.' Guy nods like a doll hanging in the back window of a car. 'We could offer a minimum of six rooms open to the public. Now about considerations for the current tenants?' Guy winks at us. Then his face falls loose. 'What do you mean? You *still* need endowment? You still need endowment after all I'm offering you? I wouldn't bloody well be giving you the house if I had any endowment, would I?' He throws the phone back to Anthony. 'Bloody sharks.'

'The National Trust have to be businessmen, that's all,' Anthony points out.

'There's more than business in life,' Melissa suddenly chips in.

'There's money, darling,' says Anthony. 'There's clothes. There's holidays. There's impressive houses. They all boil down to one thing. Money.'

'There's babies.'

'What do you mean, *babies*?'

'I'm having a baby, Anthony. *You're* having a baby.'

'Say that again. One word at a time.'

'We are going to have a baby.'

'What do you mean, a baby?'

'A little Anthony. Or Melissa. In a sopping nappy. Bawling all night,' says Guy.

'Like when? This financial year?'

'Babies aren't meant to be tax-efficient.' Melissa looks like she might cry.

Anthony is only stunned for less than a minute. Then the triumphant Anthony breaks loose again, trampling over all of us with his enthusiasm. 'I'm a bloody genius. Do you hear that, everyone? I'm going to be a father!' He grabs two more bottles from the case by the door and fills all the glasses in sight. 'Drink. Drink,' he commands, 'to my son.'

Adelaide swills the wine round her palate, not *quite* as they do on the telly before pronouncing on the touch of blackcurrant and the hint of compost, but with considerable gusto. She sighs deeply and swallows. 'A child in the house. As there always should be. Drink up, Guy,' she says, for he's staring into space. 'A child in this house after simply decades.'

'The *Siegfried Idyll*,' says Amy. 'You must play it during the birth. What better way to enter the world than to the sound of Wagner?'

'To help me relax?'

'I don't suppose it will do that. Wagner wrote it while Cosima gave birth. To celebrate the nativity of his son. All this wonderful music while she was writhing about in the bedroom. Can you get more romantic than that?'

'Without much difficulty,' says Adelaide.

Grace sits with her hands together and the candle-light exaggerates the transparency of her skin, and below it the semi-opaque creamy bones. They are a casket for an inner light. Her face is flushed with the variety of alcohol she's got down in the long wait. Dear Grace. She hasn't had access to this amount of drink since Christmas. She's watching Guy. She leans across, and touches him on the arm.

'Now a child is to come to this house,' she murmurs. 'You should tell him, Guy.' There's a new urgency in her voice. Almost a command. This is Grace unleashed by the wine.

Guy starts. 'Tell him?'

'Tell Cob, dear. *I* know, you see. I've always known. About you and his mother. Always known, but told no other soul.'

'Not the time nor the place,' Guy mutters. 'I know now it's got to be done. But in my time.'

'What's all this?' Cob and I are the only two not affected by the grape. The adrenaline within is neutral-izing it.

'This *is* the time,' says Grace. 'There can be no turning back now.' She picks up her handbag and feels inside, reassuring herself what is within. 'I must do this. I believed that God wished me to keep my counsel. But I see that's wrong now. This may not be God's will, but do it I *must*.' She turns to Guy and holds out her hands, as if offering him a gift of opportunity.

There's an embarrassed silence round the table.

Eventually Guy realizes that with all eyes on him, he has to say something. His voice is hesitant, as if he fights a grief. 'You may or may not know that David Hume was accused of having a love-child. A child he never acknowledged.'

'That won't do, Guy,' gurgles Adelaide. 'You're not thinking of having a model of the child somewhere, are you? For the dear old National Trust. In the hall perhaps. With some battered toys.'

'Stupid woman,' says Guy. He pauses for a minute to let Adelaide's crass remark fade. 'Admiring David Hume as I do, I can but conclude that he had no connection with that child at all, that there were malicious lies. However, as a rational man, I must admit to what is the truth. I *do* have a child. I intend to honour that child.'

Guy has a child? *Guy?* Bloody hell. He's joined the human race. It must be the pain of Milo's suicide, the excitement of the David Hume link, the rebuff from the National Trust, and now the miracle of a baby coming to Loughnian House. So many shocks have jolted him askew.

Guy sighs. 'A more rational man would remain quiet. This evening anyway. Perhaps I have come some small way under the influence of the great philosopher Hume, who once worked within my own library. Perhaps I stand within the illumination of his magnificent mind. Have you wondered, Cob, why I've

221

provided you with a home these last two years?'

'You said you'd made an arrangement.' Cob looks tense.

'Have you thought *why* that arrangement might be?'

'Because my mother was once a Loughnian?'

'Not that alone.' Guy's voice sounds so strange. He's having difficulty.

'Reason can't give us all the answers, can it Guy?' Cob looks him full in the face, challenging.

Guy shakes his head, confused. 'I have founded my life on reason,' he murmurs. 'On Milo's intelligence and wisdom. I know no other way.' He bows his head, a man defeated.

He lifts his head and looks up at Cob, almost beseechingly. 'I intended,' he whispers, 'to do something contemptible. I tried to ignore the truth.'

'The truth? Truth. What is truth?' Cob is scornful again, the old antagonism rising up.

'It seemed as well when you were young that you knew nothing. But I was always going to have to tell you. I was supposed to tell you when you were eighteen. I let that day slip by. What I'm going to say will give you pain.'

'Get on with it.'

'You thought your mother was married before.'

'Yes, she was.'

'I'm afraid that's not true. Your mother was never married to your natural father.'

'What do you know about that?'

'I'm your father.'

'You? *You?* How could *you* be my father?'

'Your mother was an attractive lady, and I was a lonely middle-aged man. Must I spell it out?'

'You're not my father for heaven's sake. Don't try to make that out.'

'I have the birth certificate. In the apartment. Keep it

in the safe. Obviously not something I choose to carry on my person.'

He says no more, and neither does Cob. Guy has his eyes fixed on the table, Cob's are blank and held in space.

Grace swallows hard and straightens her back. 'It's all true, my dear. I have some items for you, Cob.' She opens her handbag and takes out a photograph, and a package. 'I usually keep these in my room. I brought them tonight because with going to university you seem quite grown-up now.' She hands him the photo.

I can see, as it lies in her shaking hand, it's of three people, the photo I saw earlier in the drawer of her desk. Guy looking handsome, Grace, still very attractive, together with a younger woman, whose pale blue eyes I've seen before. She has to be Cob's mother. The same eyes as Cob, the same eyes as Milo Loughnian. It may have been a photo taken at a church fête. Behind them is a stall of cakes. Very likely some of them made by Grace.

Guy carries on. 'There's no doubt, I'm afraid. She was a lady of superficial beauty, and that was all. I can only say that neither she nor I wished to be together after one brief week. Even when she knew she was having a child. You.'

'You let her down?'

'Certainly not. It was her explicit wish she was not under my roof. Then she married the man who brought you up, and was happy. I offered financial help, but she would have none of that. For fifteen years no mention was ever made. Not even after Angelo died. Not until she was ill. Then she wrote and asked me to provide for you until you were eighteen. But she made it very clear she didn't want you under the same roof as myself. Under my influence in any way. I think she expected me to continue with the rent for the house you both lived in. But I couldn't afford that. My economic winter had already set in. Hence the cottage. I'm sorry. It's been difficult for me as well.'

'You've never liked me.'

'I didn't like your mother much either.'

'You cold-hearted sod. Your *duty*. Your duty as the *aristocrat*. You cold, bloodless man.'

'I shall support you through college.' He can't bring himself yet to say university. 'Continue my support *after* you're eighteen.'

'Support? More cold-hearted duty. Thanks. I'll get a loan.'

There's a horrible, embarrassed silence. Even Grace can find no balm to soothe.

For me, this silence, this vacuum of time, this momentary void slips. I glimpse Milo, so vivid in my mind it's as if he were here in the room. I wish he were to touch Guy's shoulder. I blink again, but he's gone from under my eyelids.

Guy says, as if he's trying to pull something out of his soul, from a long way off, 'I understand your response, Cob. I know I have to change. I must be more pleasant. I'm trying, but I've no vocabulary for kindness. Benevolence doesn't fit me well.'

I have been holding my breath, and now it sifts from me with a sense of relief. Benevolence. Benevolence, the great quality of David Hume, the generosity that Milo believed he himself lacked, is acknowledged by Guy. At last, and so late.

'Wagner's father was not his mother's husband,' says Amy helpfully. It would have been more meaningful to Cob if his father had been a Wagner fan. It seems Angelo never played Wagner, since he was not a composer to lend himself to a single instrument. Wagner needs the lot.

Cob is stunned. I hold his hand under the table. There's more to come.

'This small package,' says Grace, reluctant now, 'I was given by your mother before she died. To pass on to you at the appropriate time. I suppose this is it. I fear, Guy, that this may be her revenge.'

Cob does nothing at first. He's quiet for ages, stroking the back of my thumb under the table. I feel weird from the waist down.

No-one speaks until he *does* open it, revealing three letters. Cob picks up the first, and skims through. 'This is from my mother.' There's a look of wonder on his face. 'She says she wants me to know how I'm related to the Loughnian family. She hopes Guy will enjoy hearing what she has to say. She never told him herself because, though at first she hoped it could create a bond between them, she quickly realized it would do the reverse. She didn't want me to know of my birthright until I was old enough to fight for it. She feared otherwise it might be wrested from me.'

'That woman never changed,' says Guy. 'Trouble to the end. What's she on about now?'

Cob reads on. '"These other two letters will prove that the father of the child at whose birth Elizabeth Fraser died was Milo Loughnian. But that the child was brought up as if he were the son of Geoffrey Fraser, and in his name. Guy has extensively traced his own ancestral link with the Loughnian name, but knows nothing of the Fraser line. This type of academic study not being something I could manage, I employed a specialist in the field to do it for me. I enclose the family tree which connects me to the son of Milo Loughnian. All that is written there is verifiable in public records."'

'How can she know Elizabeth Fraser was right about who was the father?' Guy points out. 'Didn't exactly have genetic testing in those days, did they? Wouldn't have done a blood test.'

'They had as good as. There's a letter from Elizabeth to her child. She knew she was going to die. The letter was kept by a lawyer until he was adult, and kept in the family ever since. Usually by lawyers. That's this second letter.' Cob unfolds a stained and faded sheet, and reads.

'"My dearest son, I know not yet by what name to address you.

There is a truth which I must reveal to you, when you are old enough to bear it. I write now, upon the birthing bed, for I have been told that the signs do not bode well. It takes the very last dregs of my strength. The pain is staunched by laudanum, but soon I will drift into sleep. My maid will pass this letter to Mr Charlesworth, who deals with my own family legal affairs, with instructions for secrecy. To have known from the start would have hurt too greatly the man who will bring you up. This man, my husband, dear Sir Geoffrey Fraser, who suffers tragically from the war, is not your father, though he supposes himself to be, having needed the comfort of my bed despite his disabilities. Your true father is a delightful man, whom I scarcely knew, but with a very fine mind and the palest of blue eyes. He is practically my last memory of happiness. His name is Milo Loughnian, but I believe him to be too unworldly to concern himself with children. Love you he may, but I doubt he would busy himself with the practical matters of rearing. Since you will have grown to love your family father dearly, I trust this knowledge will not undermine your situation, but only enrich it.

Should you come to doubt my word, trust the

colour of your eyes. My own are blue and those of my husband brown. I cried out the name of Milo in my early birth pangs, and the midwife became my confidante. She says brown eyes will nearly always prevail. If both parents have blue eyes they never bear a brown-eyed child. Of course, all children are born with their eyes blue, but my midwife is a patient and observant woman. These matters are revealed within a year. She tells me she knows many secrets.

Whatever awaits you, my child, my last born, know that I would have loved you with all my heart.

Your sad and yearning mother,

Elizabeth Fraser."'

'How do we know that's not a fraud?' asks Guy. 'It would mean Cob is of the direct line.'

'It's the same hand as her other letter. Although a bit of a scrawl.' Cob is smiling. Direct Milo Loughnian genes compensate for the shock of Guy's share of Loughnian genes in general.

'Why didn't the wretched man, when he came of age, claim Loughnian House then? Tell me that,' demands Guy.

'The third letter explains. This one is from the lawyer, Charlesworth. He says that with their estates in Surrey and Hampshire, as well as the London mansion, Elizabeth's son James saw no reason to lay claim to the modest property in Hertfordshire so happily occupied now by Milo's younger brother. *Your* ancestor, Guy. He also observes what a charming man James is, such kind blue eyes and gentle, studious manner.'

'So the upkeep of this *modest* property is your responsibility. Is that what these letters say?'

'I wouldn't live here at any price,' says Cob. 'I want to live in a round house, made of glass. With no

227

pockets of the past. No dusty corners. And I want to earn my own crust. I want to make a difference to the future.'

'Good man,' says Guy. 'Got your head screwed on. Like I'd expect my son to have.'

Amy says, to stop the evening deteriorating further, 'I've made *my* decision. I'm *not* going back to Henry. It wouldn't be right.' She opens her full dry mouth, and her teeth gleam at us with all the lights reflected back from Anthony's chandelier. 'Now let's have coffee.' She leads the way to her apartment fairly steadily.

Almost before we're settled down in the conservatory, Guy says, 'We'll see how this year goes. If I'm forced to sell to this man from the gutter, this James Wright, I shall see you ladies financially safe.' Then he adds, some of the generosity sliding off the offer, 'It's what Milo Loughnian would have done.'

Anthony says, 'It doesn't have to come to that. I'll make you a further offer, Guy.'

'Put us out on the street so you can get your greasy little hands on the stately home. Is that it?'

'Things have changed, Guy. I have children to consider. Education. Boarding-schools are simply *out*. Passé. A first-class day-school is what you *must* have. Get a decent nanny and they won't be any more trouble than packing them off. Got to get the area right, of course. Vitally important, the area. Kensington, I imagine. Possibly Hampstead. Does anyone know if nursery-schools have league tables? I mean, it's crucial for a toddler to mix with his peers. We'll get advice on that tomorrow, Melissa.'

'What exactly are you saying, Anthony?' Adelaide's as confused as the rest of us.

'I'm saying that I shan't want to *live* primarily in this house for a number of years. Happy to keep the apartment as a country retreat. But for the future. A splendid home for the boys to come back to from Oxford. Impress the other rugby blues. Think of the daughters coming down that staircase in their wedding dresses. A slice of their own history. Classy. What's in it for me, you ask? If I buy it now, it's a sound investment. Still a fairly depressed housing market. This way it can stay a home for Guy, and the older ladies for as long as they're around. No offence meant, but that won't be for ever. How does that grab you, Guy?'

'I couldn't bear this place to have a pool. With a Jacuzzi.'

'Rest assured, Guy. No pool. Remember, there's style but there's also breeding. That's what I've got to provide now. Breeding. Lineage. Heritage. They won't come cheap either. We shan't be having anything flash. Get all the furniture into the proper rooms first of all. You could have a bedroom upstairs again, Guy.'

'The one where David Hume slept?'

'I don't have a problem with that. This is where you people come in useful, of course. Eccentricity about the place. Sign of the aristocracy. Hang on to your old sweaters, Guy. Change the colour of your wellingtons. Throw out the acrylic cardigans. I'm looking to an ongoing aroma of shortbread from you, Grace.'

'You may wish me to advise on the furnishings,' Adelaide offers.

'You'd have to discuss that with the lady of the house.'

'What about the library?'

'Yours till you reach the great reading-room in the sky.'

'You've got it made, Guy,' says Adelaide.

'There would have to be written conditions. Strict, clear conditions. Quite a lot of them.'

'Of course. Of course.'

'Then I *may* go to my solicitor in the morning. After all, eighteenth-century affluence *was* beginning to come from trade as well as land-owning.' Guy says nothing more, but there are tears on both his cheeks. I'm pretty certain they're of relief, not pain.

'Splendid,' bellows Adelaide. 'That couldn't be more marvellous. Absolutely everything is marvellous. I'm so happy for you all.' She leans heavily and uncontrollably against Guy. The future looms before her. Secure at last. A man to drink with, but no messy obligations. The apartment no longer about to slip from her grasp. Adelaide is a woman content.

Grace sits silently, fingering the collar of her blouse, occasionally giving a small nod, almost confident.

Amy stands at the cooker, pouring water over coffee grains, straining them through a muslin. Concentrating on the gurgle of steaming water, she looks more ethereal through the screen of potted plants. Still and intent, illuminated by light reflected from the wall behind her, wild hair thrown into relief, elephant-grey eyes without expression, there's mystery enveloping her. An aura of potential joy. Laurie watches, as if committing every feature to memory 'I love this place,' she says. 'I *love* it.'

He realizes I'm watching him. 'There's the Celt in that woman, you know. As a woman should be. Full of poetry. Imagination. You'd take her to be Welsh.'

My heart soars for Amy. She's ceased to hope, and she shouldn't have. However, I shan't pass on the bit about the Celt in the West.

'Cheer up, everyone,' calls Adelaide, subsiding further down the chair, head level with the table top now.

Coffee made, Amy thumps the jug on the table, and sweeps away into the sitting-room. She collects the phone and sprawls on the sofa, dialling the numbers with stabbing, energetic urgency. I'm certain she's ringing Henry. It's Amy who does most of the talking.

Eventually she replaces the receiver, sits up cross-legged in the middle of her sofa, still and tranquil once more. The sofa and Amy are as one, complementary extremes, formality and freedom, safety and creative energy, order and chaos. Only one lamp is lit in the sitting-room now, and it illuminates my aunt among her cushions, bathing her in limelight. Only *she* exists in that room, all around her are unimportant shadows. She radiates warmth, from within herself, from her nature, from her heart. Her benevolence spreads out among us like yeast through bread.

Amy and I smile at each other through the window between sitting-room and conservatory.

In that moment, Laurie starts to hum. I wonder what the sound is at first. A deep, resonating hum. Vaguely I recognize the tune as something Amy often plays.

Then he sings. A rich baritone, passionate, powerful, the voice of the Welsh valleys. I can scarcely believe his choice. How did he know to pick Wagner? '*Dich frage ich*' from the *Der fliegende Holländer*. The Dutchman is standing on the shore, asking if the torment of searching for the love of a true woman will end. Only this can save him from another seven-year stint on the high seas.

Amy's mouth drops open. Luckily she quickly shuts it, and gives herself over to listening properly. She closes her eyes, and sways minimally with the music. It's as if the room dissolves around her, leaving only Amy, luminous and central to our lives.

Laurie takes off his glasses now, leans against the conservatory door, singing only to Amy.

I wish this moment could be eternal. Not only because Amy is happy, but because I could listen to the exquisite sound for all time. Its fear and its hope is the allegory of my own life too.

231

Now Amy smiles. Her whole face moves, eyes, mouth, even her nose. That's never happened before.

Anthony says, 'That dirge won't get into the top twenty.'

Later, when the evening comes to an end, Guy gathers up his Milo and Hume letters, and, as he passes Cob, brushes his hand across his shoulder. Shy and tentative. 'You've done well,' he manages to get out, in little more than a gruff whisper.

Laurie deliberately puts his spectacles on the table before leaving. Obviously he didn't hear Cob whisper to me, 'You'd better see me home.'

Chapter Twenty-one

Cob and I walk round the house several times, content to be within its circle of warmth. For so long this house has been doomed, but now it lives again, Anthony its saviour. The Philosopher's House will be safe. No-one will lose their home. It will not become a pathetic ruin, nor be flattened to make way for a modern estate. The house will hold within its walls the many strata of time, the intangible imprint of other lives, the ethereal past. Milo will perhaps become famous now, through the house appearing in *Homes and Gardens. Vogue* would take it on, provided Melissa featured prominently. Anthony may be so eager to show off his restored historic splendour he might even open the House to the public. Not because he'd need the money. Just to show off. Be his own mini National Trust, with postcards of Milo's portrait, a booklet of his letters, extracts from his journals on table-mats. Small prints of Amy's painting of the Italian garden. Anthony will need to think well ahead here. I'm sure he will if he wants to use Milo to his own advantage.

The burden of exam results has fallen away. Got a new problem now. I'm scared of what we both know is to happen next. Perhaps Cob is too. Walking is all we ever do. No cinema. No trips to the pub.

In the Street-Langtons' extension there's a light on in the upstairs room where Melissa put the cot. In the square of bright light she and Anthony are laughing, their arms around each other. Melissa is making her nest, and has swept Anthony into it.

Melissa pulls away, unentwining herself. A symbolic move. She's shed her protean skin, and will no longer vary her style to suit Anthony's prevailing whim.

'They won't be living here much longer. Only visiting.'

'In London they'll appear quite normal,' says Cob. 'Anthony will change with his orientation. Ever the chameleon. His image will shift between tycoon, intellectual and country gentleman. Only those with time on their hands will know he's a man whose veneer goes all the way to the core.'

We turn the corner and come across Amy walking purposefully towards the studio apartment. She's humming Senta's song, her song of redemption and healing for the Dutchman. Except she has a Welshman in mind just now. I recognize it. Amy giggles when she sees us, and says, 'Laurie left his specs.' She knocks on Laurie's door. 'He might be lost without them.'

'Come in,' says Laurie. 'Please.' He's not at all surprised she's there.

Amy peers into the room, and sees the fruit bowl with its wonderful yellow sunflowers in pride of place on the table. It's heaped with lemons.

'You've put it out.'

'I didn't think you'd want it any different.'

'*I'd* want it any different?'

'This being where you should be living, Amy.'

'What about you?'

'You're not really getting me, are you?'

'I'd never dare. I mean, I wouldn't presume. Oh dear,

234

I don't mean that either.' She takes a deep breath. 'What I mean *is* I like things spelled out good and clear.'

'Being so artistic and intuitive and perceptive and spiritual and all that?'

'Yes, but you're not.'

'Try me.'

'Perhaps I am beginning to get you, Laurie.'

'Not beginning to get, Amy. Got. Good and proper. I'm not shifting.'

'Looks like Anthony will have the conservatory sooner than he expected,' says Cob.

We pass the dim glow from Grace's kitchen where she makes bedtime cocoa, to comfort the two ladies in their tormented night, driven by lusts and fantasies. However, a few minutes later, as we pass the front of the house, Grace crosses the hall and knocks on Guy's door. She hands him a mug of cocoa. Grace was born to be a handmaiden. A psychiatrist would say she'd got a Martha and Mary complex. As she walks back, her expression is of pure exhilaration, almost divine inspiration. Grace is a fulfilled woman. By Christmas she'll be cooking Guy's meals as well. Amy's dream of a commune will be more fully realized than she could ever have hoped.

Amy's windows show no light at all, but, across the courtyard, closed curtains filter the soft lights of the studio. No shadow moves across them. No conversation leaks out into the night.

We end up here, in the Italian garden. It's more beautiful than it's ever been before. There's a benign breath informing it. If I believed in a God I'd think he were here. There's some force for good in this place, willing happiness. Perhaps even *our* happiness.

Cob moves across, very close, nearer than he's ever

235

been. I feel shy, so unready for what might happen. Almost frantically I prattle, 'Stoa. The summer-house. Stoics. Good lies in the state of the soul.' So long as I continue in conversation I won't have to do anything, or say the right thing.

Cob moves away from me. He's more nervous than I am. 'Lucretius was called the Philosopher of the Garden. Perhaps a garden just like this.'

Now I'm scared that nothing at all will happen. I've gone and blown everything. Again.

'What did Lucretius say?' I ask, mesmerized like a mouse in the eyeline of a cat, unable to move, unable to stop babbling.

There's a pause, almost a soft breeze moving through the garden, and Cob moves close to me again. 'He said the supreme good is pleasure.'

I can breathe normally again, as we lie on the floor of the summer-house. I have become a woman. I know the *Ultimate Experience*. I have lived.

Not altogether certain what all the fuss is about. Perhaps it gets better with practice. All I could think about was poor Cob, getting in such a state. Those haunted blue eyes. Now I know Cob has Loughnian genes, I saw his eyes were just like Milo's in the portrait. For a moment I pretended he *was* Milo Loughnian, and then the *Ultimate Experience* didn't seem quite so uncomfortable.

I remember the falling leaf I caught on the second day I saw this house, my gift of one happy day. I'm going to university. I have become a woman. I am fulfilled. Sort of. The leaf has kept its promise.

In the night, I disentangle myself and look out through the window of Cob's cottage towards the house. The moon lights everything, and I can see its face smiling down on this world. The house is as grey as the first time I saw it, but no longer cold. It's breathing and alive. It will be happy again. *Everything* tonight is benign.

I no longer need to live within the lives of others. I have a life of my own at last. I have gathered myself. I have borrowed from nearly all the people I have met in this house. We are a jigsaw of our circumstances. Sometimes we can rearrange the pieces. I think of David Hume's heart bubbling over with generosity the way that Amy's warmth bubbles out too. This is the way I want to be. Each morning I shall look within myself and find the warmth. It's an art. It's a craft. One day, it will be me.

I don't need religion, and I don't need philosophy. I will not be taught, but I *will* learn. Learn from history. There's so much history to which I can listen. This house, Milo, ancestors never met, our parents, and the great swirling of thought, whose pattern, like the foundation-stones of ancient villages, can only be distinguished from a distance.

The shadows in the surrounding shrubs dance as the clouds pass over the face of the moon. As if there's someone there. There *is* a man there. He steps out from the shadows and strides across the grass, down to the drive. Once he turns and looks at the house. I close my eyes and can still see him, the frock-coat with ruffles at the neck, lace at the wrists. Eventually he fades away, like the Cheshire cat.

Milo is free. Because benevolence and love prevail here now.

Today I have to go home. Mother arrives back from Corfu. She'll be in a state over Nick. I shall walk to the station and get the earliest train. My mother needs comforting. I shall be there. Though she's rarely been there for me.

Who will Cob meet in Sussex? I hope one day, Cob, you'll love a big-hearted woman, who will make you joyful. Who will make you sing. As Laurie sang last night.

Who will I meet in Durham? I can't think about that, I can't imagine the future at the moment.

I can't live in the past either, but I know for certain it will always be there. The current may have washed beyond my plank of the bridge, but, though I can no longer see it, the same water still gushes against other stones.

The past is a wise song, and its music should always be playing.

THE END

Holy Aspic

Joan Marysmith

'PARTICULARLY ASSURED WRITING'
Daily Mail

A delightfully funny and poignant novel of
provincial life.

Fenn Meadowcroft, beautiful, vague and a
wonderful cook, is battling with a crisis of faith.
Somehow her conventional beliefs no longer seem
enough: why is her ineffectual schoolteacher
husband so dull, life so unsatisfying, and the
vicar's weekly sermon so nonsensical? Her
daughter Damaris, having failed her A levels, is off
to Australia on a worryingly disorganised trip with
Marie, the daughter of Fenn's next-door-neighbour
Dodo. By contrast Doug, Fenn's louche and
entrepreneurial cleaner, boasts of his son's success
in gaining a place at Oxford. For Fenn, life seems
empty and unfulfilled.

Small wonder, then, that she falls easy prey to
Dodo's enigmatic new lodger Lex, while Dodo, her
own eye firmly on Lex, fails to notice that her other
neighbour, frail and elderly May, is losing her grasp
on reality. Initially reduced to hiding in the
fishmongers to avoid the vicar, Fenn discovers
other ways of filling her time . . .

'A GENEROUS HELPING OF WRY HUMOUR AND
TENDER CONCERN . . . SOME LOVELY,
MEMORABLE TOUCHES'
Woman and Home

0 552 99688 2

BLACK SWAN

A SELECTED LIST OF FINE WRITING
AVAILABLE FROM BLACK SWAN

99766 8	**EVERY GOOD GIRL**	*Judy Astley*	£6.99
99722 6	**THE PULL OF THE MOON**	*Elizabeth Berg*	£6.99
99687 4	**THE PURVEYOR OF ENCHANTMENT**	*Marika Cobbold*	£6.99
99755 2	**WINGS OF THE MORNING**	*Elizabeth Falconer*	£6.99
99770 6	**TELLING LIDDY**	*Anne Fine*	£6.99
99795 1	**LIAR BIRDS**	*Lucy Fitzgerald*	£6.99
99760 9	**THE DRESS CIRCLE**	*Laurie Graham*	£6.99
99611 4	**THE COURTYARD IN AUGUST**	*Janette Griffiths*	£6.99
99774 9	**THE CUCKOO'S PARTING CRY**	*Anthea Halliwell*	£6.99
99778 1	**A PATCH OF GREEN WATER**	*Karen Hayes*	£6.99
99736 6	**KISS AND KIN**	*Angela Lambert*	£6.99
99771 4	**MALLINGFORD**	*Alison Love*	£6.99
99688 2	**HOLY ASPIC**	*Joan Marysmith*	£6.99
99689 0	**WATERWINGS**	*Joan Marysmith*	£6.99
99701 3	**EVERMORE**	*Penny Perrick*	£6.99
99696 3	**THE VISITATION**	*Sue Reidy*	£5.99
99747 1	**M FOR MOTHER**	*Marjorie Riddell*	£6.99
99506 1	**BETWEEN FRIENDS**	*Kathleen Rowntree*	£6.99
99663 6	**GARGOYLES AND PORT**	*Mary Selby*	£6.99
99781 1	**WRITING ON THE WATER**	*Jane Slavin*	£6.99
99753 6	**AN ACCIDENTAL LIFE**	*Titia Sutherland*	£6.99
99700 5	**NEXT OF KIN**	*Joanna Trollope*	£6.99
99720 X	**THE SERPENTINE CAVE**	*Jill Paton Walsh*	£6.99
99723 4	**PART OF THE FURNITURE**	*Mary Wesley*	£6.99
99761 7	**THE GATEGRASHER**	*Madeleine Wickham*	£6.99
99591 6	**A MISLAID MAGIC**	*Joyce Windsor*	£6.99